Snow One Like You

Also by Natalie Blitt

Carols and Crushes

Snow One Like You

Natalie Blitt

SCHOLASTIC INC.

For my dad, Peter Blitt, in gratitude for a million BeaverTails and every-thing, everything.

Chapter One

Usually, when my first alarm clock goes off at six a.m., I ignore it. It's all part of my wake-up plan, my perfect recipe for a chill and stress-free morning.

First alarm: "Here Comes the Sun" by The Beatles. It's quirky and sweet, and it never fails to put a smile on my face. And not just because it's my dad's favorite song.

My second alarm clock goes off exactly ninety seconds after the first song ends. It's carefully timed: just enough silence to allow my brain to slowly wake up, but not enough to do what it really wants to do, which is go back to sleep.

Alarm number two is another happy-go-lucky, classic song—"Daydream Believer" by The Monkees—but it's definitely more upbeat, and impossible to sleep through.

The third alarm is the local Top 40 station. Knowing the DJ's obnoxious voice will blare out at me after "Daydream Believer" is usually enough incentive to make sure I'm up out of bed and shutting it off. Particularly since that alarm clock is on the other side of the room.

But this morning, like every morning for the past week, my system falls apart. I do wake up calmly to The Beatles, but as soon as the song's over, I switch off The Monkees alarm. Then I dash out of bed to where the Top 40 alarm rests on my desk, shut *that* off, grab my phone, and jump back into bed.

It goes against all my rules, and as a result, I've been cranky and late to school all week. But I can't help it.

I slide under my heavy duvet, turn on my phone, and tap the weather app.

Please, please, please, I beg the universe as I wait for the app to show the ten-day forecast. I even have a ritual for this part. I squeeze my eyes shut and count to five while picturing piles and piles of fluffy snow.

Maybe—

I open my eyes.

Nope.

Zero percent chance of snow over the next ten days.

My heart sinks.

I open the six other weather apps that are taking up my phone's memory. I check them all, even the ones I know aren't terribly reliable.

Except, there's still no snow in the forecast on any of the apps.

And no snow in the forecast means . . .

"Mia, are you awake?"

It's really quite amazing how my mom is able to project her voice up the stairs and yet never seems to be yelling. Unlike me. Half the time my best friend, Lark, says I sound like I'm yelling when I'm trying to talk softly into the phone.

I jump out of bed. I might not have noticed the cold when I darted out to grab my phone, but now that I'm not distracted by my prayers for snow, it's all I notice. I shiver in my pajamas.

If it's not going to snow, couldn't it at least be warm?

"Mia?" There's a note of irritation in Mom's voice, and I try not to let it bother me. We're all stressed out. "Alice isn't coming in until later, so I need to be at the front desk now."

I breathe in and out a few times. I love living in the little cottage behind the Rocking Horse Inn. My great-grandparents originally ran the inn as a boardinghouse, but by the time my grandparents took over, it had already been transformed into an inn. The building, which is well over a hundred and fifty years old, is a large, redbrick Craftsman-style structure that houses twenty rooms; a dining area; a kitchen that's run by my stepdad, Thierry; and a study filled with old books. It also has a fantastic wraparound porch that is the best place to read six months out of the year.

Normally, in the winter, the whole inn looks like a movie set, with the twinkling lights we hang across the porch and fresh white snow blanketing the roof. But when there's no snow? It looks and feels cold and desolate. Kind of like an old building with poor heating and well-worn wood accents.

"Mia Buchanan!" Mom calls.

But the major problem with living on the inn's property? There's no division between home and work. Mom and Thierry are constantly running between our small house and the inn across the garden. It can get a little crazy, especially in the high season.

"I'll be ready in a couple of minutes!" I promise. "I'll meet you at the front desk."

A couple of minutes is probably a lowball estimate, but if I told my mom I'd spent the last fifteen minutes trying to find a weather app that might suggest the possibility that there could be some snow in the next ten days, there'd be more than a hint of irritation in her voice.

I grab the first pair of striped tights I find in my drawer—brown-and-turquoise, one of my favorites—and fling on a jean skirt, a black T-shirt, and a thick, dark purple sweater. They don't really go together, but I'm too late to be mixing and matching outfits. I quickly go through my bathroom routines, grab my backpack, and pull on my coat and boots. Then I make my way across the freezing tundra between our house and the inn, trying to walk and French braid my long brown hair at the same time. I resist the urge to grab my phone out of my coat pocket and check the weather apps *again*, just in case they might have changed since I woke up. I know. I'm obsessed.

Though, to be fair, these days, everyone in my town of Flurry, Vermont, is similarly obsessed. The "will it snow or won't it snow?" discussion seems to be the *only* topic of conversation. We all want to know whether the snow will come in time to save Flurry's Winter Festival.

Every year since 1855, the town of Flurry has held the Winter Festival the weekend before Christmas. Part pre-holiday party and part craft fair, the festival takes over our downtown area as thousands of people descend on our little town from all across the country. To people who've never been to the Winter Festival, it doesn't sound like one of *the* main events in the state of Vermont. But something special happens that weekend. No one can put their finger on what it is exactly, but everybody who comes to the festival leaves in high spirits. It's almost . . . magical.

That, and it's responsible for a good chunk of the money the entire town economy depends on.

And while the festival may be a ton of work, it's also a ton of fun. There's a cross-country ski event for kids under five (I won that race when I was all of three years old) and a cross-country skiing marathon that is every bit as exciting as the New York City Marathon (so I've been told). I first learned to build a snowman at the festival when I was four. And I've always, *always*, participated in our attempts to break the world record for the "Most People Participating in a Snowball Fight" snowball fight. Even the year I had the flu. *And* the year I broke my arm the day before the festival began (that's why you have two arms, I insisted). In my family, the festival is bigger than Christmas and the Fourth of July put together.

And while I love the festival every year, *this* year is extra special.

On our living room wall, there's a series of photographs, each with one person smiling and waving from a horse-drawn sleigh. The first picture features my grandfather, the next my grandmother, and after that, my mom.

Each of them, the year they were in seventh grade, had the coveted honor of being the junior coordinator of the Flurry Winter Festival. The junior coordinator gets to ride through town at the end of the festival in a horse-drawn sleigh while the entire town watches and cheers.

The junior coordinator is always the head of the seventh-grade student council, who, this year, is me. As long as everything goes right, in less than two weeks, there should be a fourth picture in the lineup, with me on that glorious sleigh ride.

Except, if there's no snow, there's no festival. And if there's no festival, there's no need for a junior coordinator, which means no sleigh ride and no photograph. It's not like I can try for the position next year: This is the only year. And it's what I've been dreaming of since I can remember.

There needs *to be snow*, I think as I let myself into the inn. There needs to be a Winter Festival. And I really, really need that sleigh ride.

"Mia, the school called yesterday and said that it would be a problem if you had another unexplained late start," Mom says from behind the antique table that functions as our front desk.

Even this early in the morning, my mom is the picture of elegance. Not in an obnoxious way. She doesn't flaunt expensive clothing or look falsely made-up. It's more how she holds herself, calm and collected, her dark hair swept into a small bun at the nape of her neck, a soft burnt-orange sweater tucked into a pair of chocolate-brown pants. People always say Mom and I look alike—same brown hair; same lanky frame; same pale, freckled skin. The only difference is, Mom has brown eyes, and mine are blue. Also, I don't think I quite inherited her beauty or poise.

"I'll be on time," I tell Mom, carefully picking an apple out of the giant glass bowl that sits on her desk. I've become quite the expert in removing fruit from that bowl without getting my fingerprints on the glass.

"Honey, you need a more substantial breakfast. Go ask Thierry for something with protein," Mom tells me as the phone rings. I watch as she steels herself, puts a smile on her face, and answers the telephone like it's her favorite task.

The person calling can't see how tired she is, how she pinches her mouth together as she listens.

I know what's happening. It's what's been happening all week.

"Unfortunately, we really don't know when the snow will come, Mr. McAllistair," Mom says, and I sigh. "The town has yet to make a decision about what will happen should there not be any snow, but I promise you, we'll call all of our guests as soon as we know. However, if you'd prefer to cancel your room, I would understand. That said, we do have a waiting list, so it's unlikely that we'd be able to reinstate your reservation should you change your mind . . ."

I slip away before she finishes the call. I don't wait to find out what Mr. McAllistair's decision will be. Chances are, he'll keep his booking until the last possible minute before canceling it. Guests usually do, since it's so difficult to get a reservation in the first place. We've actually taken to publicizing the date we start taking general reservations for the Winter Festival months in advance. If we don't book up the day reservations open, we're always booked by the next day. This year, though, it seems like all those reservations might turn into cancelations, if the snow doesn't show up.

Stuffing the apple into my book bag, I walk into the big, airy kitchen. While the inn's foyer is neat and perfectly decorated—not unlike my mom—the kitchen is a warm chaos of smells and tastes. Just the way my stepdad likes it.

"Good morning, Mia!" Thierry calls from where he

stands at the stove. Thierry's lived in America since he and his family came over when he was in high school, but the warm timbre of his voice still reflects his childhood in Haiti.

"Morning, Tee," I reply with a smile, making my way toward him.

My stepdad is big and strong, with a shaved head, dark skin, and sparkling eyes. He's one of the most comforting people in the world. His body is built up from lifting massive quantities of food all the time, carting huge pots of soup and oversize pans of oven-roasted chicken. I remember once offering to help him carry something from one end of the kitchen to the other, and I quickly learned that what he makes look easy is difficult for most ordinary mortals.

"Strength doesn't come from here, *chérie*," he told me once, pointing to his bicep. Then he'd placed his hand over his heart. "When you have the love of your family, you can lift anything."

Now Thierry smiles at me. "I have an egg and cheese burrito ready for you. It's even all wrapped up so you can eat it on your way to school." He winks, and I roll my eyes. Thierry and I might not share the same DNA, but we do have the same propensity for "not being good at time management" as Mom likes to say.

I give him a quick hug, accepting the burrito in its tinfoil wrapper. It smells delicious, but I'm distracted.

"Tee," I whisper, "are people really canceling reservations because they think there might not be snow?"

He frowns and shrugs one shoulder. "I think people are worried," he allows, but he doesn't really meet my eyes. "For many families, coming to Flurry for the festival is their big trip during the winter. Since the festival is so dependent on snow for all the activities, I think some people might wonder if they should skip making the trip this year."

My stomach clenches, and now it's my turn not to meet his eyes. I was hoping Thierry would say something reassuring. I thank him for the burrito, wave good-bye, and head out the kitchen's back door to the main road.

It's not that Thierry told me something I don't know. All

the activities that make the Winter Festival unique completely revolve around snow.

As I walk to school, munching on my breakfast burrito, I run through the list in my head:

(1) Cross-Country Ski Marathon

(2) Snowshoe Race

(3) World's Biggest Snowball Fight

(4) Snowman Building

(5) Sled Building

(6) Competitive Igloo Making

They all need snow, and more than just a dusting.

My breath comes out in puffs as I cross the street. Sure, it's cold enough to still skate on the pond, or even go ice fishing. The artists and artisans will be able to set up their craft booths, and the food trucks and snack stands will be open, hawking hot cocoa and roasted chestnuts. But that's not really the festival.

The festival is an old-fashioned celebration of snow. It's what Flurry, Vermont, is known for, why people choose to come here, why our family's inn has stayed in business for so many years.

So what Thierry said is true.

If there's no snow, why bother coming to Flurry at all?

Chapter Two

I wait for my best friend, Lark Mapp-Jefferson, by the main entrance of the Elizabeth Stanton Middle School. Contrary to Mom's expectations, I managed to arrive before the first bell. True, it's the first time all week, but I'll take what I can get.

It helps that it's only a ten-minute walk from the inn to school, so if I don't stop to admire the decorated porches and shop windows in town, I can cut a few minutes off my usual time.

Flurry is small enough that, were it not for the Winter Festival, we would be some forgotten town, probably not even listed on most maps. Instead, by virtue of the festival, we're not only included on maps, but also on websites that promote "The Ten Most Picturesque Towns in the Northeast" or "Top Five Hidden Treasures for Winter Break Travel."

Most houses and buildings in town are protected by the historical society, which means that Flurry looks like the set for some charming TV show. The buildings are intentionally distinctive, their shells colorful and bright. They make for fabulous pictures when they're surrounded by fall leaves, spring flowers, but especially bright white snow.

Which reminds me.

I tug my phone out of my pocket, and check the weather apps again.

0% CHANCE OF SNOW.

0% CHANCE OF SNOW.

0% CHANCE OF SNOW.

0% CHANCE OF SNOW.

0% CHANCE OF SNOW.

0% CHANCE OF SNOW.

0% CHANCE OF SNOW.

I frown. What was I expecting, anyway? I'm quite sure that the weather isn't controlled by my dependence on weather apps.

Lark's mom's Prius pulls up in front of the school, and I jump off the low wall where I'd been perched. Lark's family car is distinctive because of the FLURRY MAYOR decals.

Soleil, Lark's mom, began the practice of labeling her car when she became the mayor, saying that she wanted to be accessible to the people in town. I wonder if, after the past few weeks of nonstop worry about snow, she's still happy to be so easily identifiable.

"Morning, Soleil," I call from the sidewalk as Lark gets out of the car.

"Morning, Mia!" Lark's mom calls back with a cheerful honk.

"Don't ask about the festival," Lark hisses, stuffing her pale hair under her pom-pom hat.

"I wasn't going to," I lie, and turn back to the beat-up Prius. "Have a great day!" I yell. "Keep fighting the good fight!"

I sound like an idiot.

"Seriously?" Lark says to me as her mom drives off. "Keep fighting the good fight?"

"I couldn't think of anything else," I admit. We turn to head into school together.

While I tend to be a fast walker, walking with Lark forces me to slow down, which has the additional benefit of relaxing me in general. Lark was born with cerebral palsy, which in her case mainly affects her legs. As a result, it takes her longer to walk from one place to another. The way she explained it to me is that she uses 50 percent more energy to walk than your average person, which means that if I'm walking five hundred steps, it's as if she's walking seven hundred and fifty just to get to the same place. Since we've been friends forever, I don't even think about it anymore, I just walk slower.

As soon we step into the bustle of the crowded school corridor, Lark whips off her ski hat, exposing her wet hair.

"Swim practice?" I groan. I can barely get out of bed for *school*. I can't imagine having to wake up at five to get into the pool of all things.

"Yup." Lark never seems to mind the early morning practices. "I shaved an extra second off my best time today!"

We high-five. "But isn't today a rock-climbing day?" I ask.

"Yup. But I missed swim practice last week when I was out of town for the climbing competition, so I had to make it up this week."

People who don't know Lark may look at the way she walks, the positioning and shape of her legs, and assume she can't do much. The truth is, she's one of the most athletically driven people I know. I get tired just listening to her schedule.

We head to our lockers in the East Bay, saying hi to the other seventh graders that pass by. Most kids don't even notice anymore that Lark walks differently, or remember that she used to wear plastic braces around her shins and ankles before her surgery, though they are more careful around her. They know to try to avoid accidentally bumping her.

We reach our lockers and Lark turns to me, her gray-green eyes dancing.

"So, maybe today will be a good time for you to say something to Yoshi," Lark says as she spins the dial on her locker. "Like, at the student council meeting."

"Say *what* to Yoshi?" I whisper, my face heating up. I mess up the combination on my own lock.

"Um, maybe drop hints that you like him?"

"Shhhh!" I glance around in a panic. I can't believe that Lark is saying this stuff in the hallway.

Because we're such a small community, I've known most of the kids at Elizabeth Stanton Middle School since we started kindergarten, if not before. Yoshiki Pennington—or Yoshi, as he asked us to call him—is one of the most notable exceptions. He and his parents moved to Flurry from San

Diego this past summer. I've gotten to know Yoshi because we were paired up as lab partners in science class. He's *so* California, and *so* not Flurry: He wears a necklace made out of shells, and his backpack has different surfing patches sewn on.

But he's sweet and funny and, well . . .

I might have a teensy-tiny little crush on him.

Maybe.

It's just that I sometimes get kind of swoony when he runs his hand through his shaggy, longish black hair. Or when he smiles.

But we're just friends. That's all.

"Come on," Lark says. "I was speaking so quietly, I'm surprised you could even hear me."

"I could hear you just fine," I mutter. "Anyway, I didn't say I definitely had a *c-r-u-s-h* on him. I said I *might* have a cru—I mean *c-r-u-s-h* on him."

Lark giggles, and I grab her arm. Because her balance isn't top notch, if Lark starts laughing too hard, she often falls down. Which tends to just make her laugh harder. "You know that anybody who might overhear our conversation knows what *c-r-u-s-h* spells."

I smirk. "I know that. It's just that I'm used to spelling things out when I talk to Dad and Shannon in front of the littles. Especially when it involves food they might want. Like *d-o-n-u-t-s*."

The littles are my three little sisters. Well, my half-sisters. My dad married Shannon a few years after he and Mom divorced, but it took a few years until the littles came along. Talulah and Tabitha, the twins, are both three, and Lilou, the baby, is eighteen months. They are my favorite kids in the world.

"Anyway," Lark says in a slightly louder voice as we start to walk to our first-period history class. "I'm just saying that you might want to actually tell *Y-o-s-h-i* how you feel. Because maybe he feels the same way."

"Seriously?" I give her my best death stare. "You know I'm not brave enough."

Okay, so assuming I *did* have a real crush on Yoshi, I can't imagine what it would be like to actually *tell* him. What if he *doesn't* feel the same way? What if it makes things awkward between us? What if he likes someone else, and because I confess that I have a *c-r-u-s-h* on him, he doesn't want to spend time with me anymore? What if—

"I can't even hear your thoughts, and I'm already feeling like I might have a panic attack," Lark whispers to me as we enter our classroom. "Fine. You don't need to say anything. Sorry I brought it up."

"Thanks," I say as we reach our desks at the front of the room. "So," I add, changing the subject. "Is there anything new about the festival?"

For a long moment, I wonder if Lark didn't hear the question because she doesn't even react. But the strength with which she drops her backpack on the floor makes it clear that she did. "Mom says they're going to call an emergency town council meeting," she finally replies. "Basically, if there's no snow in the forecast, they need to make a decision about canceling the festival."

My stomach drops. They can't cancel the festival. They just *can't*.

"But there's always the chance that—" I start.

"Mia, come on," Lark says, a little more harshly than I might have expected. She sits down at her desk beside me and gives me a serious look. "If the choice is between having people show up to the festival expecting to do all the regular things and there's nothing to do, and canceling the festival and hoping those people decide to come back next year, the town is going to choose to cancel."

No! "But what if there's snow at the last minute?" I argue.

"What if there isn't? Look, it's not like my mom wants to cancel the festival. She knows the cost of canceling it. Heck, she'll probably be voted out of office if she does. Or there'll be a riot."

For a second I try to imagine a riot in Flurry. Bari, who

runs the bakery, would probably be at the forefront, as she is with anything that happens in this town. And then behind her would be my dad with his long hair and guitar, and my stepmom, Shannon, with their three daughters strapped to her body like a super woman. And Mrs. Sollinger wouldn't care about the issue; she'd just be handing out cookies to those protesting because she loves a good ruckus. Mr. Han—my old dance teacher—would push Mr. Erickson along in a wheelchair, like he always does. And Mr. DeShawn, our art teacher, would be making the most beautiful protest signs imaginable. The image of this entire crew shouting en masse downtown creates such a funny picture in my head that I can't help it—I snort.

I catch Lark snorting, too, and I know she's imagining the same scene. "Mrs. Huang would make them all wear sashes, wouldn't she?" Lark struggles to say between cackles.

"And she'd bring Mr. Brekelmans into it, because he'd be in favor of reusing fabric sashes instead of paper signs."

"'Reusing is always better than recycling,'" Lark imitates, and then we're laughing so hard we don't hear the bell signifying that first period is about to start. But then hordes of students start rushing to their desks and our teacher, Dr. Pascal, walks in.

"I know it's a hard decision," I whisper to Lark before the lesson starts. "I'm sure your mom is stressed about it."

Lark nods. "We just need to hope for the best. Let's try not to worry too much, okay?"

"Good plan," I say.

But sticking to that plan seems impossible. At our student council meeting that afternoon, it takes about three-and-a-half seconds before the topic of the snowless Winter Festival comes up.

"I heard there's a good chance the whole thing will be canceled," Marcus Andelman grumbles, slumping into his seat.

Once upon a time, Marcus and I were best friends. You can see the evidence in the countless pictures of baby Mia and baby Marcus holding hands, splashing in wading pools together, and sleeping side by side. I was devastated when he and his parents moved away to Springfield, Illinois, before first grade. But that was a long time ago. And apparently, between first grade and last summer when Marcus came back, a lot has changed. There's nothing that remains of the little kids who posed together with their gap-toothed smiles.

Especially after I won the position of class president in the spring. After he lost that election, I was shocked that Marcus even applied to be on the student council. Although, now I wonder if he did it just to irritate me.

But my job is to treat the whole council like a team, so I can't yell at Marcus like I want to. I take my seat and flip open my laptop.

"From what I understand, a decision hasn't been made yet," I say, trying to keep my anger out of my voice. "So we still need to work on our part of it."

Our seventh-grade class is small, so the student council is small as well: it's just me, Marcus, Lark, Yoshi, and Kyle Jones, a short, friendly boy whom I've known since preschool. We all sit together in a circle in the study room of our school library, and most of the time, we get along pretty well.

Maybe not today, though. "But if there's no snow, we can't have a festival," Marcus says, giving me a look that tells me he knows exactly how much he's getting to me. "Any chance there's snow in the forecast, Yoshiki?"

I glance at Yoshi across the circle, trying not to blush. I can feel Lark watching me with a small smile.

Yoshi gives Marcus a barely concealed eye roll. "No, Marcus. My dad hasn't given me any top secret information that he hasn't shared with the viewers of WVVW."

"It's a shame," Marcus drawls, and I don't know if he's trying to imitate Yoshi's California accent or just being annoying. "Since your dad is the weatherman, you'd think you could score us some good news."

"You know meteorologists don't create the weather, right, Marcus?" Yoshi snaps back.

Before things can get more heated, Maayan Lerner, school librarian extraordinaire and the seventh-grade student council adviser, sails through the door. Today she's wearing a 1950s-era, twirly maroon skirt with a fitted, dark yellow sweater. Paired with her short, blunt cut and her black cat-eye glasses, she's basically the coolest adult I can imagine.

"Sorry I'm late," she says, dropping a stack of books on the table. "I got distracted looking at new books."

That's another reason I love Maayan. I know librarians are supposed to like books, but she takes it to a whole new level. One that I'm definitely down with.

I start leaning forward to get a glimpse of the books in her pile, but Lark elbows me.

Right. Don't get distracted by the pretty books.

"Okay," I start. "We're at T minus ten days until the festival, so let's focus."

Every year, the seventh-grade student council gets to choose an event to run at the festival. Back in September, I had petitioned not to take an event that already existed, but to bring back an older, forgotten event. I'd really, really wanted to do something cool and unique for the festival. So the student council and I worked up a proposal for bringing back the Snow Carnival, which was last held more than twenty years ago. It was really fun, with different games and booths. But . . . the town council said no.

So instead, we took on Snowman Building. And I might be going a little crazy with it.

"Yoshi?" I say, lifting my chin. "Can you update us on how the costumes are coming?"

Yoshi nods, his dark brown eyes bright. "I've now been to every Goodwill, Salvation Army, and thrift shop within twenty miles of here and"—he glances around the room—"I have an awesome assortment of costumes, including cool hats, scarves, and sunglasses."

"Nice going, man," says Kyle. Lark claps, and Maayan pumps her fist in the air.

"Thanks, Yoshi," I say, feeling a beat of excitement. I turn to the spreadsheet I've pulled up on the laptop and make a notation. "Lark?"

The student council and I decided to ramp up the Snowman Building event this year. Sure, the die-hard builders are going to bring their carvers and molds and whatever other tools of the trade they usually get. But we wanted people who aren't professional snow carvers to be able to participate, too. I got the idea from watching an episode of the TV show *Gilmore Girls* (because seriously, Lorelai and Rory's snowman was the best). Festivalgoers will be able to construct a basic snowperson and then dress them up with things like old pocket watches, feather boas, monocles, and purses.

But the most exciting part, and the one that Lark is now updating everyone on, is the photo booth. Lark and her dad created a backdrop made of tie-dyed fabric and four poles, which can be placed behind the snowpeople. Festivalgoers can pose with their creations, and we'll encourage them to post the pictures on social media. And Lark's started creating all the fun accessories that accompany real photo booths, like handheld signs and fake, oversize glasses. We bought a few selfie sticks and I think the whole thing will be a total blast.

"Thanks, Lark," I say, nodding at my best friend. "Marcus and Kyle, how are things going with the booth itself?"

Marcus and Kyle are in charge of the construction of the actual booth, as well as the signage.

Marcus shrugs. "I didn't get any paint yet."

"Ms. Mackenzie gave us the wood from woodshop," Kyle adds helpfully.

"You guys need paint, Marcus," I point out.

"My dad will take me to the art supply shop to get paint this weekend," Marcus replies shortly.

"Remember to keep your receipts so your dad can get reimbursed," Lark pipes up.

Marcus makes a face and Kyle looks apologetically over at Lark. Kyle got the raw end of the deal in the committee assignments, having to work with Marcus, but I did that on purpose, knowing Kyle would keep him on task.

"My dad can handle the cost," Marcus mumbles.

"Well, we do have a budget," Lark says. "And I've been pretty careful with how we're spending stuff, so there's money for paint if you need it."

I debate whether to remind Marcus that materials were supposed to be purchased by last week. And that he'd told us he'd already bought them when we met last time.

"I don't really see the point of buying stuff until we know for sure that the festival is happening, do you?"

I let his sentence hang in the air and then decide I'm just going to pretend it's a rhetorical question.

The rest of the meeting goes by with relative ease. As everyone is leaving, I spend a few minutes with Maayan, making sure there's nothing I missed.

"You did a great job out there, Mia," Maayan tells me with a smile. "You allowed Marcus to have his say, but moved on when the conversation wasn't going in the right direction."

I feel a rush of pride as I return her smile. Maayan's praise means a lot to me.

"Are you excited to be Flurry's junior coordinator at the festival?" she asks, and I blush hard.

I don't want to tell her that it's my dream come true. I know it's not really that big a deal, that people hire horses for sleigh rides all the time. But there's something magical about the fact that you can only take this particular sleigh ride if you're the student leader. Twenty-six years ago, it was my mom in the sleigh, her hands kept warm with an adorable fake-fur muff. Forty-eight years ago, my grandmother had that spot, and fifty years ago, it was my grandfather. Mom said it wasn't important whether my photo joined theirs or not, but it feels like destiny at this point.

Which is reason number one billion that they can't cancel the festival.

"Very," I admit.

Maayan winks, causing her glasses to shift up and down on her nose. "I would be, too," she says. "And I know all your hard work will pay off."

Chapter Three

I practically skip out of my meeting with Maayan. I'm so caught up in my little, happy bubble that I almost don't notice Lark, Yoshi, and Kyle hanging out by the front doors of the school.

"Okay, what's the epic grin for?" Lark asks, jolting me out of my reverie.

If it were just Lark standing there, I'd admit it to her, because she definitely knows how I feel about the sleigh ride. But with Kyle and Yoshi there?

"I'm just really looking forward to our Snowman Building event. I mean, what could be better than getting to decorate your snowperson, and then posing for pictures?" It may not be the real reason I'm grinning, but it's not that far from the truth.

"I can think of a few better things," Kyle points out with a small smirk. "Like never having to take a test for school again? Or winning the lottery?"

Lark swipes a hand across his arm. "Kyle! Don't be difficult," she teases as we head out into the cold.

The two of them start walking down the school stairs, and Yoshi and I wind up trailing behind them. I'm envious of how easy it is between Lark and Kyle. Sure, they've known each other forever. But I keep trying to tell Lark that Kyle has a crush on her, which she denies. If she could see the way he's looking at her right now, though, she'd have to agree. If only I could take a picture so I could show her . . .

That would definitely be awkward.

And speaking of awkward, I wish I could think of something to say to Yoshi. He's walking beside me, his hands in his pockets, his dark hair peeking out from his wool ski hat. I wonder what he's thinking.

Lark turns around. "Oh, listen. Kyle has an hour before he needs to meet his dad, so I told him he could wait at my place. Yoshi's going to come over, too. Any chance you want to join us?" she asks me. "We were going to work on making more props for the photo booth . . ."

Lark and Kyle and me and Yoshi? My face heats up. It seems really double datey. I try not to look at Yoshi. Maybe this is Lark trying to force my hand.

But I can't really say no to designing props . . .

"Sure." I nod.

Anything for the good of the festival.

Right?

At Lark's house, Kyle heads down to the basement to collect some art supplies, and Lark, Yoshi, and I get settled in her living room.

There's a lot to look at. Lark's dad is a climber, and there are framed pictures all over the walls of the different places he's been and the photographs he's taken. I know them all by heart, but Yoshi is seeing them for the first time.

"These are amazing," Yoshi says. "Did your dad really take these?"

"Yup," Lark says. "All climbs he's done. All his photographs." I'm sure Yoshi doesn't know that this is the millionth time Lark has heard the same comment.

"Lark actually took the one in the corner," I point out with pride. The photograph is just as spectacular as the rest, with the beginnings of a sunset lighting the mountaintops.

Yoshi glances at me, his brows furrowing like he's not sure whether I'm joking.

"Seriously," I say. "Lark's an amazing climber, too."

"But . . ." Yoshi's voice trails off as he stares at Lark's thin legs. Then he looks over at me with a guilty expression on his face.

"You know my policy," Lark says, no anger in her voice. "If you have a question, just ask. It doesn't offend me."

Lark's dad, Chris, comes in with a tray of hot drinks, and Yoshi takes a half step back. Chris is tall and broad in his blue flannel shirt and jeans, his messy red hair and beard just a shade too long. Chris and my dad rock a similar hippie-ish look.

"Um, so how long have you been climbing?" Yoshi asks Lark, clearly not the first question on his mind, but the only one he feels comfortable asking.

"Since I was six?" Lark glances up at her dad, who nods.

"Right, because you'd already been climbing for a good amount of time before your surgery," Chris adds.

Yoshi's eyes turn to mine, and I give him a little nod to reassure him he isn't stepping on any toes.

"Many climbers use their legs for power," Chris continues, "but because Lark's legs can't give her the power and stability she needs, she uses her arms."

"I've got good guns." Lark winks, pointing at her biceps under her sweater, and I crack up.

"That's really cool," Yoshi says, still looking embarrassed.

"He should hear the story about when you climbed that wall after your surgery," I tell Lark. It's one of my favorite Lark stories because it's so perfectly Lark.

"You start, Mia," Lark says, taking a mug of tea from her dad and sitting down in a chair.

"So, about four years ago, Lark had this major surgery on her back," I begin.

Yoshi frowns, his gaze moving to Lark's back, like there might be something he didn't notice.

"They went in through my back, but it was really for my legs," Lark explains. "It's complicated."

I nod. "Anyway, there's this huge climbing wall outside of town that Lark climbed every summer. She'd been able to get to the platform at the top without a problem before the surgery—"

"I wouldn't say without a problem," Lark says with a smile. "But I could do it."

"And then six months after the surgery, she went to the same climbing wall. Nobody thought she'd be able to do it again, not yet. The whole town came to cheer her on. But she started going up, and we were all yelling and encouraging her . . ."

I drift off because it's one of my most powerful memories. Seeing Lark struggling but determined. Soleil and Chris standing at the bottom, their hands clasped together. And there was Lark, steadily climbing the wall, one handhold and foothold at a time.

"We all figured there was no way she could do it," Chris takes over. "She'd just had this major surgery, and it seemed impossible. But Lark was determined. Except, she got up about eighty percent of the way, and she stopped climbing."

"The plan had always been that if I couldn't get to the top, it was no big deal, I'd just keep working on it and try again later," Lark says, her gray-green eyes bright with determination. "But that was not going to happen. I'd done this climb every year, and I didn't care if I'd had surgery or whatever. I was climbing that wall. I was not letting them bring me down."

"And that's what she yelled from the almost-top of the wall," I say, the memory of Lark's bravery making my voice quiver. "She was yelling and crying, saying: 'Do not bring me down! Do not bring me down!'"

Lark shrugs and gives me a little wink. "And I did it."

I remember. Everyone was crying. The whole town had come to see her succeed at whatever she'd be able to manage. Nobody had thought she would get to the top of the climbing wall. But she was that committed.

"Okay, that was a fun stroll down memory lane, but I've got to get back to my office," Chris says, kissing the top of Lark's head. "Give me a holler if you need anything else to drink. You may be able to climb mountains, but I don't want you carrying hot liquids."

Lark rolls her eyes. "As if I'd do that."

"It's a balance thing," I explain to Yoshi as we sit down on the couch. "Lark usually has a fifty-fifty shot of getting a drink from point A to point B without spilling it."

"Fifty-fifty is generous," Lark corrects, and I roll my eyes right back at her. .

Kyle emerges from the basement then, carrying craft supplies, and he brings them over to Lark to examine.

"You okay?" I whisper to Yoshi.

"I just feel dumb," Yoshi mumbles. His long bangs flop over his forehead, and he pushes them back. But the bangs just land back in his eyes.

"Hair tie?" I offer, pulling out one of the half dozen elastic bands I keep in my pockets.

Yoshi glances up and chuckles, his fingers swiping mine as he takes the band. I feel a jolt of electricity shoot through me, and then his fingers are gone and my heart is beating out of control. Yoshi seems oblivious, though, as he pulls his bangs back again and this time fastens them behind the crown of his head with a few flicks of the elastic.

"Don't feel dumb," I say, keeping my voice quiet to slip under the sounds of Kyle and Lark discussing crafts. "Unless you've lived here forever, you wouldn't know that story, or that Lark is way more athletic than anyone would believe. But she really doesn't get offended when people ask. The only thing she hates is when people stare and don't ask."

He nods, not meeting my eyes, but then tilts his chin toward me. "Thanks," he whispers, and it's like the feeling of his fingers brushing mine. It makes me shiver.

And judging from the smirk on Lark's face when I glance up, she saw it all.

I'm in for a world of teasing. But somehow, even that doesn't bother me right now.

It turns out Yoshi is a genius when it comes to creating cardboard facial hair. I'm jealous. My mustaches are cartoonish and uneven, and my beards look like giant brown triangles. In the time it takes me to carefully trace out the pattern that Lark copied onto the paper, Yoshi's done two or three mustaches and fixed the ones I ruined.

"I give up!" I laugh when it starts taking him longer to fix mine than to make his own. "You're so much better at this than I am."

"You just haven't hit your groove yet. There's still time." Though, in the space it's taken him to get out those two sentences, he's created a pointy green beard.

"I'm going to work on glasses with Lark and Kyle," I say, getting up from the sofa.

"No!" Yoshi implores. "Don't go to the glasses side." I know I shouldn't read too much into this statement, but my heart feels jumpy.

"Don't listen to him!" Lark shouts from her chair from a couple of feet away. "Come to the glasses side. We have cookies!"

"You have cookies?" I ask, even though I know it's just a joke. The dejected sigh that Yoshi levels at me makes the whole thing worth it.

Luckily, the doorbell rings before I have to make the difficult decision between my best friend and Yoshi. Though, if she could get a plate of cookies, it wouldn't be much of a competition.

But now Kyle's leaving, and his dad agrees to take Yoshi home as well. And just like that, it's me and Lark.

"So, did you say anything to him?" Lark asks as we clean up the art supplies. We have a nice pile of props for the photo booth, but that isn't what's making me feel warm and fuzzy inside. "There seemed to be some good flirting going on."

"Flirting?" I echo. "No way." But I think of how I felt when Yoshi's fingers brushed across mine. Still, he must not have noticed.

"What if he doesn't like me like that?" My voice is quiet because I hate even thinking those words. Especially since I'm almost positive they're true.

"What if he does?" Lark asks in a much louder voice.

"It's too much of a risk." I shake my head. "Plus, things looked pretty flirty between you and Kyle. Did you talk to *him* about it?"

"Nothing is happening with Kyle," Lark says, and before I can say anything more, she says the magic words: "Any chance you're in the mood for making cookies?"

"How was your day, girls?" Soleil asks when she gets home and joins Lark and me in the kitchen. She has dark circles under her eyes, and while her tone is friendly, she's not her usual exuberant self. She's clearly exhausted.

"Mom, sit down," Lark says, pointing to the chair. "I was about to take the chocolate chip cookies out of the oven."

"You were . . ." Soleil frowns at Lark.

Lark makes a face. "I meant Mia will take them out. Don't worry."

Soleil puts her hand on her daughter's. "I can't help it. I'm worrying about so many things, it all just spills over."

The oven dings, and I jump off my chair to grab the cookies. Maybe if I hang around long enough, Soleil will let something slip about the festival.

I put on oven mitts and carefully remove the tray from the baking rack. Lark helps me set the tray out on the table to cool, and I shut off the oven.

If Soleil wasn't here, I'd get ice cream to go with the cookies, but that seems like a little much before dinner. At least in front of a parent.

"Oh, just grab the ice cream, Mia." Soleil sighs, scraping off a bit of cookie and blowing on it to cool it. "If we're going to indulge, let's go all out."

Lark gives me a subtle thumbs-up. Apparently, tired Soleil is more likely to be fine with ice cream and cookies before dinner. Good to know.

Lark, her mom, and I all dig into vanilla ice cream topped with still-hot, mushy chocolate chip cookies. Lark and I have been eating this concoction since we were too young to make our own chocolate chip cookies. But it's only a Lark's-house thing. No chance Mom and Thierry would ever go for anything nearly this junky. And Dad and Shannon would never have all the right ingredients at their place.

"How's the Snowman Building station coming?" Soleil asks us.

"It's going to be epic," I say, my mouth full of chocolate. "I'm telling you, this will be the best festival ever."

"I hope so," Soleil says. "Right now, I'd just settle on knowing whether we were having the festival or not."

I freeze and look at her for more information.

"Half the folks here think the town will fall apart if we skip one year," Soleil explains, "and the other half think the town will fall apart if we have a less-than-perfect festival. Which means we're at a standstill."

The kitchen goes silent, and Lark doesn't meet my eyes.

"Well, hopefully you won't need to make a decision because it'll start to snow!" I say, and Lark rewards me with an impressive eye roll. Okay, I should have kept my mouth shut, but Soleil knows I'm not just one of her constituents. She's practically my godmother.

"I wish it was that easy," Soleil says. She allows her spoon to drop in the sink and walks out of the kitchen.

Sorry, I mouth at Lark, but she gives me the eye roll again. And now I'm not feeling as warm and fuzzy as I was a minute ago. That, and the chocolate chip cookie goop is starting to churn in my stomach, which means I should probably go home and take some Pepto-Bismol.

Chapter Four

The walk from Lark's house helps me clear my head a little. There will be a festival, I know it. We just need to have faith that the snow will come.

I enter the inn the way I left, through the kitchen, mostly so I don't get in trouble for tracking in mud. I know that Mom's been overwhelmed by the anxiety of guests possibly canceling, so I'm trying extra hard to fly under the radar.

The kitchen is empty, but I can hear Mom and Thierry talking right outside in the hall. I pause, listening.

"Well, one thing that would help is if you could start creating menus that are less dependent on individual portion sizes." I can't see Mom, but the tone of her voice suggests that she's close to losing her cool. Except, Mom never loses her cool.

"Amy, *chérie*. It will be okay." Thierry's voice is lilting and soft, just like always. If I had to guess, I'd say that his over-size hands are framing her tired face.

"No, Thierry," Mom says, a sigh embedded in the words. "You make amazing food, and it's one of the big reasons that our guests stay with us. But these days, everything is so precarious. We can't be wasting food if our reservations change."

Her voice is getting higher pitched, and I chew on the side of my thumb. The inn serves breakfast every morning and a traditional dinner every Saturday night, in addition to the extra meals we provide during the festival. Saturday dinners include waitstaff and cloth napkins, and the tables are set with the good china. That's part of the reason I spend Saturday nights at Dad's house: Mom and Thierry don't think it's fair to put me on display at dinner in front of guests. When they have friends for dinner, that's one thing.

But for "Inn Dinners," I'm happy to spend the time with Dad, Shannon, and my little sisters.

"Amy, I try as best I can to make food that will easily stretch and that freezes nicely. But I'm a chef. I can't serve lasagna or stir-fry to our guests if you want them to continue paying for these meals."

I've never heard this level of exasperation in their voices. Mom and Thierry don't usually argue.

"But this is a really serious situation," Mom says. "I don't know where else to cut from—"

"I get it," Thierry interrupts.

"No, you don't. I did look into what it would take to sell the inn, but I really hate the idea."

I'm straining so hard to hear the rest of her comments that it takes my brain a few minutes to catch up.

Sell the inn?

"I talked with Sarah Beth Hart at Plymouth Realty about other inns in the area to get a sense of how much we could expect to see," Mom is saying. "Because this is a historic building, she thinks that we should be able to get a nice sum. But then we'd need to find another place to live . . ."

"*Chérie*, we can't think like that yet."

"Thierry, we have to. Especially now that they're talking about canceling the festival. We're counting on that income . . ."

I can't listen anymore.

. I back out of the kitchen and reenter the cold outside. I feel even sicker to my stomach than I did before. I knew we'd been having cancelations and that finances were tight. But I didn't think it was this serious.

If the inn were Dad's home, I wouldn't worry. Dad's a dreamer. He and Shannon manage to make ends meet, even though they live in a tiny log house in the middle of nowhere with three kids under three, and neither of them work full-time. Some weeks they just have less.

But Mom's not like that. Not that she needs more, but she's a planner. She doesn't let herself get into a position where money isn't coming in regularly. She believes in college funds and stability.

And right now, there's none of that.

I stand outside in the cold, blinking back tears.

We can't lose the inn. We can't leave Flurry.

How would I go back and forth between my mom's and dad's houses? How would I see Lark? And what about other friends . . . like Yoshi?

I manage to gather myself together enough to go back inside the inn. If I bump into Mom or Thierry, I don't want them to see me so upset, to know I overheard them.

But now more than ever, I know that the Winter Festival has to happen. This one weekend is a huge financial boost to the inn every year. And there must be something I can do.

I'm seriously dragging when I get to school the next morning. I stayed up late researching weather patterns, and then when I couldn't understand most of it, I started looking up other winter festivals online. Because it can't be that ours is the *only* festival being affected by changing weather. Maybe not this winter, but other festivals in other years . . .

I came up with a short list of other festivals that have been affected in the past, but that didn't prove very helpful. Some canceled (not an option). Others postponed (also not an option given that Christmas is the following week). And others just dealt with ice sculptures that melted too quickly, or skating rinks that couldn't be open for the festival.

But nobody dealt with our particular issue of having a festival dedicated to snow . . . without snow.

So now I'm sleep deprived and discouraged. And when you add in late for school? Well, I should wear a sign that says STAY CLEAR.

Especially since the forecast still shows no sign of snow. Showers, yes. Because that's what we need. Rain.

I try to keep my head down, but it's hard when rumors

are swirling through the school, picking up steam with every new person they pass through.

The festival is definitely going to be canceled! (I'm pretty sure Lark would tell me if that were true . . .)

The town has declared a state of emergency. (Really? Is that even possible?)

The Rocking Horse Inn has lost all of its bookings for the festival. (Almost positive I'd know if *that* were true.)

"Stop listening to them," Lark side-whispers to me as we make our way down the school corridor.

"I'm not," I lie, though I know I'm not fooling anyone. I'm walking slower than Lark, and that never happens. "But you'd tell me if the decision to cancel had already been made, right?"

When there's no answer, I quicken my steps to face her. "Lark, you'd tell me, right?" My voice is doing that oh-so-attractive squeak, but I don't even care.

Lark steps to the side, out of the movement of the crowds.

"No decision has been made," she reassures me, staring me straight in the eye. I nod slowly, because I know she wouldn't lie to me. Not with something this important. "But you saw my mom last night. You need to prepare yourself for the very real possibility that they'll need to cancel the festival."

"No." I shake my head frantically. I glance up to stop the tears that are already hovering. There are holiday decorations all over the school. Even though Flurry's a small town, we're made up of people who come from so many places and identities, and our school's walls reflect that. There are decorations for Christmas and Kwanzaa and Hanukkah, along with paper cutouts and illustrations of people of all ethnicities and family makeups.

I love this school. Well, as much as one can love a middle school. And I love Flurry. But if there's no festival, and Mom and Thierry decide to move . . .

I can't even bring myself to tell Lark what I overheard. Not yet. That would make it too real.

"It needs to happen," I say. "It just does." My voice is loud enough that it draws the attention of everyone around us. Luckily, that's when the bell rings, and my outburst is quickly forgotten.

I spend the day brainstorming creative solutions for the festival while I pretend to be interested in what my teachers are saying. Can we import snow? Can we generate machine-made snow like ski slopes do? Or maybe we can change the starting day from Friday to the following Monday so we can buy ourselves more time? But each idea is as impractical as the last. By the end of the day, the only thing I'm convinced of is that I can't do this by myself. If only because I apparently lack the imagination for it.

Luckily, we have a student council meeting set for that afternoon. Maybe together, we can brainstorm a good idea for what the festival could look like if there's no snow.

Marcus, Kyle, Lark, and Yoshi are already in the study room when I make it to the library after the last bell. Mr. DeShawn held me back in art because he, correctly, could tell I was making no effort at all. But when he saw my tears welling up, he let me go pretty quickly.

"Maayan came by and said we should start without her," Lark reports when I walk in. "She had to run to a last-minute staff meeting."

"Okay," I say. I wish Maayan was here to help calm my nerves, but I'll do the best I can.

I stand in front of the room, clasp my hands, and try to give off a sense of calm and authority. Ha.

"Hi, guys," I begin. "We all know that rumors are going around that there's a chance the town might decide to cancel the festival."

I pause for dramatic effect, but nobody really seems to be reacting, so I power on, only slightly daunted by their silence. "So, because we've done such an epic job reimagining Snowman Building into something totally awesome, I thought we could take on another project." I take a breath and continue. "Welcome to Operation Save the Festival! All we need to do is figure out how we can convince the grown-ups in town not to cancel the whole thing."

I smile widely, like this is some sort of fun adventure that we're all embarking on together. Everyone, even Lark, just looks at me like I'm a little crazy.

"Think of it like one of those movies," I go on hopefully, "where the kids have the opportunity to save the day! So the question at hand is, how can we have the famous Flurry Winter Festival if there might not be snow in time?"

There's still no word from the others. I try smiling again, but I think that might be scaring them. "Please," I whisper, taking the enthusiasm down a few notches. "I can't imagine not having the festival. We know that the businesses in town need the festival. And the festival is such an important event in all our lives . . ." My voice trails off, and I plop into an empty chair. "We need to find a solution."

"We shouldn't be interfering with it," Lark finally speaks

up, her tone firm. "It's not like the town council *wants* to shut it down. They don't. But they need to think about what's best for the whole town. Not just this year, but for future years. If they keep the festival on, but half the activities are closed because there's no snow, nobody will come back next year."

"If we cancel this year, it's entirely possible we won't be here next year," I shoot back. *Well, I won't,* I think sadly.

Lark narrows her eyes at me. "Wait, *what*?"

I take a tight swallow, and at the last minute, I fudge. "I didn't mean anything in particular. Just that the town depends on this money, and many businesses will suffer if the festival doesn't happen."

Her eyes stay on me as though she's trying to catch me in the lie. But this isn't the time to tell her about what I overheard last night.

"None of us want to skip the festival this year," Kyle jumps in, looking around the room. "But what can we actually do?"

"We're in middle school," Marcus says with a shrug. "At best, most of us remember the past five or six years of festivals. Our parents remember dozens. And some of them even remember coming as kids. We need to let the adults in town make this call. We can't step in."

My tears are making it hard for me to see people clearly, but at least I don't think anyone can tell that I'm crying. Yet.

"We need to *try*, though," I argue.

"Mia is right. We should do anything we can to help," Yoshi says, and I feel a flicker of relief. "But we should be strategic about it. There's going to be an emergency town council meeting, right?"

"Yeah," Lark confirms.

"Why don't we find out what's needed after that?" Yoshi suggests. "And then we can spend our time brainstorming wisely. For all we know, it won't even be necessary. Maybe the grown-ups have a plan."

"And if they don't?" I snap. The fact that it's Yoshi making these comments is transforming my sadness into anger.

What does he even know about the importance of the festival to this town? His parents don't run businesses that will be affected. This town will always need doctors like his mom and weathermen like his dad.

Not like my family's business.

"Then maybe it isn't solvable." His voice is gentle, which infuriates me. "Some things just can't be saved."

His words hang in the air around us, but nobody pushes them away. Nobody tells him that he's wrong, that the festival needs to be saved at all costs. Lark won't even meet my eyes.

"Fine," I whisper, hating how my voice cracks. The tears are so close to overflowing that I have no choice: flee or have everyone see me cry.

So I take the only real option. I grab my bag and speed walk out of the library. I stop by my locker to get my coat and scarf, then I head for the school exit. At least I have a whole weekend before I have to see anyone again.

Chapter Five

"Mia, wait!"

I'm halfway out the school doors when I hear Yoshi running up behind me. But I refuse to turn around.

"I get it. Not everything can be saved," I say bitterly, still walking quickly ahead, out into the cold. "You made your point."

I'm not going to outrun him, so instead I turn the corner of the school and lean against the brick wall. It's not like I think that he's going to run right past me like in an action movie, but it would be a nice gift. Especially since today has basically been the pits.

Yoshi doesn't even need to slow down; he takes the same turn I did and then stops where I'm standing. He's just in his sweater; he didn't stop to get his jacket, and he hugs himself to keep warm.

"I really don't want to talk about this anymore," I tell him.

"Listen, I don't know if we can save the festival," Yoshi says, his gaze intense. "But I also know what it's like when you feel hopeless. So I'm happy to help you in any way I can."

The chill is deep in my bones, and for a moment, I wonder if the cold is making me hear things wrong.

"I thought you said we should wait until we know what the grown-ups need?"

Yoshi's shoulders rise and fall quickly. "I mean, it's probably the smart move. But there's no harm in coming up with options in advance. Since there's such a time crunch and all."

I stare into his dark eyes, but I see no hint that he's just trying to placate me. "You know my mom owns the

Rocking Horse Inn," I start. His eyes are on mine, and he gives me a tiny nod, as if to say *go on*.

So I do, because I have to tell someone. And if I can't tell Lark, who am I going to tell? "It's been in our family forever," I explain. "But lately, some of our guests have been canceling, and last night I heard my mom say that if things don't improve, if all the guests cancel that weekend, then we may have to . . ."

I'm not even sure I can get the words out.

"Well, let's just say the town really needs a successful festival," I finish instead. I try to swallow the lump in my throat.

But Yoshi seems to have read between the lines, because he takes a step closer. "I'm sure if you told Lark what's at stake, she'd do everything she can, too."

"I don't want to add to her stress. It's hard enough having the mayor as your mom. I don't want her to worry about whether we'll . . . about me."

"Well, we can do it just the two of us," Yoshi offers. "I'm probably a good person to brainstorm with because I have no expectations about the festival, and maybe I can help you think outside the box."

It's almost completely dark now, and I know that as soon as we move away from the outdoor lights of the school, we'll barely be able to see each other. I wish I knew for sure why he was doing this, whether he really does care or if he just feels bad for me.

Either way, I'm grateful.

"Thank you," I whisper. This feels like an important moment. Like it's filled with possibility.

"Were you planning to walk home?" he asks hesitantly. "Because maybe we could start brainstorming as we walk?"

I feel my heart skip a beat. I turn back to the lit-up school. I should go in there and tell Lark I'm leaving. But . . .

"I told Lark that I was going to walk you home," Yoshi says. "I hope that's okay."

I nod. I'm glad that the near-darkness is hiding my blush.

"I'm just going to go inside to grab my jacket," Yoshi adds, his teeth starting to chatter. "There's only so much cold a Californian can take."

"Yes, don't get hypothermia on me now!" I laugh, shooing him inside the building.

"Be right back," Yoshi says, and darts inside.

As I stand there waiting for him to return, my stomach leaps with hope and nervousness.

Yoshiki Pennington might be my new favorite person in the universe. I just hope I don't totally embarrass myself.

"Okay, so let me get this straight," Yoshi says as we walk along. He's trying not to laugh. "When you were six, you set up a stand in front of the inn selling sno-cones?"

For the last half hour, I've told Yoshi about all my favorite memories of the festival, which meant we needed to circle my neighborhood several times in the cold. And now we're back at the entrance of the inn. Again.

"Yup. And I made ten dollars."

"But who buys sno-cones in the middle of December?" Whenever Yoshi tries hard not to laugh but doesn't succeed, tiny little dimples appear in his cheeks. I've never seen anything that cute. Ever. I'm trying to appear cool and collected, but really, I'm melting into a pile of mush.

"Well, until Mom discovered what I was doing, it was mostly guests at the inn who thought it was adorable that I was carving up ice with my Snoopy Sno-cone Machine," I explain. "That, and they felt sorry for me because it was really cold."

Mom had almost lost it when she discovered what I'd been up to. But Thierry? He just laughed and laughed.

"Please tell me there are pictures," Yoshi begs, and I wink.

"I might be able to hook you up."

His eyes widen, and I'm suddenly mortified. Because I'm clearly flirting with Yoshiki Pennington.

Oh. My. God.

I'm flirting. Like, actually flirting.

And Yoshi and I are friends. And I don't want to mess with that.

My cheeks heat up, and I cover them with my mittened hands. But Yoshi seems not to notice because he's staring up at the inn, his head tipping back to take in the full view. "This place is amazing. You really live here?"

I forget sometimes that he's new to town. But he's right: The Rocking Horse Inn is amazing. I lift my gaze so I can see what he sees. And while the property is so much prettier when it's covered in snow, I have to admit that it's still pretty spectacular.

"Well, I technically live in the little house behind the inn. But, yes, I do."

"I can see why . . ." He pauses and clears his throat, looking away from the building for a moment. "I can see why you need the festival to happen. This is a really special place."

I blink hard to make sure the tears don't come back. I want to tell him that my mom grew up here, that the room where I sleep is the one she slept in as a child. But I feel silly talking about a piece of property as though it were a member of the family.

"Um, do you want to come inside? I can give you a bit of a tour. I mean, not of my house because my mom and stepdad are probably in the inn working, so I can't . . ."

I'm full-on babbling. Is it weird that I just invited him for a tour of the inn? Does it sound like I'm boasting? Or like I'm trying to get him alone? Or . . .

"I can't right now," he says, and I feel a mixture of relief and disappointment in my chest. "I need to get home. Can I come back another time?"

Another time. There'll be another time. Hope flares. I nod, trying to appear nonchalant.

I realize that I don't remember where Yoshi lives. It's odd: At school, we spend a lot of time together, especially with the student council and the festival coming up. But I don't know all that much about his life outside school.

"I can't remember where you live. Is it nearby?" I ask.

"My mom's office is a few blocks away, and I can catch a ride with her."

I think back to what I know about Yoshi's parents, which again is really not that much. I should ask him more, but before I can speak up, he's made his way down the path to the sidewalk.

"Do you mind if I text you later so we can brainstorm?" He's stopped to pull out his phone and his look is expectant.

I gulp. This is totally normal. Totally. Normal. Nothing to freak out about.

I tell him my phone number, and he taps it in, and a moment later I hear the ping of an incoming text.

Unknown Number: Hey! ☺

Mia Buchanan: Who is this?

I don't dare look up. What if he thinks I'm totally ridiculous or . . .

Unknown Number: Your partner in Operation Save the Festival.

I need, like, an hour to come up with the right GIF, something that gives the appearance of nonchalance and a bit of excitement. My heart is racing and I finally give up, raising my eyes to a smiling Yoshi.

"Oh," I manage to joke. "I thought it was my grandpa or something. Like, maybe he finally learned to text."

Yoshi cracks up and gives me a wave as he walks away. "Talk to you later."

He texts at six forty-five p.m., a full hour and seventeen minutes after I started staring at my phone. It's not like I couldn't text *him*, but I couldn't think of a good opener. I'm a dork.

Yoshi Pennington: Hey! Remember me?

I put his name into my phone, of course, but I can't resist teasing a little.

Mia Buchanan: You mean Grandpa?

Yoshi Pennington: Ouch! I hope that's not my new nickname. Anyway, aren't we the same age?

Mia Buchanan: Depends. When's your birthday?

Yoshi Pennington: If I tell you mine, will you tell me yours?

My stomach is going crazy. It's like a billion butterflies hatched inside.

Mia Buchanan: If you're lucky!

I smile to myself. Flirting is . . . kind of fun. In addition to being terrifying.

There's a long pause, and I have to force myself to breathe in and out.

Yoshi Pennington: February 14th

My heart jumps.

Mia Buchanan: Really?? You were born on Valentine's Day?

Yoshi Pennington: Yes. Good job on recognizing the date. #eyeroll

I giggle out loud. This is literally the best thing that's happened this week.

> **Mia Buchanan:** Well, you're older than me. My birthday is February 29th.
>
> **Yoshi Pennington:** Wait. Leap Day? For real?
>
> **Mia Buchanan:** Yep.
>
> **Yoshi Pennington:** No wonder you called me Grandpa. You're what? Four years old?
>
> **Mia Buchanan:** Har har har. Good job on figuring out the math.
>
> **Yoshi Pennington:** Well, you're very smart for your age, too!
>
> **Mia Buchanan:** My turn to #eyeroll. I celebrate my birthday on March 1st when there isn't a leap year. It's more annoying when I have to tell people my birthday because they freak out like I told them I have six toes on one foot.
>
> **Yoshi Pennington:** OMG. You have six toes on one foot? That's so cool!!!

I perch up on my windowsill and get comfortable. Because I hope this conversation doesn't end anytime soon. I don't have a good reply for Yoshi, so instead I stick out my tongue and take a quick selfie. I send it before I have a chance to really think about it. As soon as it's gone, I wish I could reach into the phone and pull it back out. Mom always tells me that I should think for a while before sending any picture via text or over the Internet.

Mia Buchanan: Feel free to delete that picture.

The thing about texting is that it isn't as fast as conversation. So for people like me who get anxious over everything, there's a lot of room to get anxious between texts. Finally, Yoshi responds.

Yoshi Pennington: I like this picture! I like your curtains.

I glance over at my curtains. The ones I've had up in my room since I was little and never got around to changing. I hadn't realized that he could see them in the photo.

Mia Buchanan: Don't mock the Powerpuff Girls.
Yoshi Pennington: Never.

And then Yoshi texts a picture of himself, standing beside *his* curtains. They are pink and floral. And Yoshi is making the same tongue-out, kooky look on his face as I did. While managing to look adorable, of course.

Mia Buchanan: OMG.

Yoshi Pennington: They came with the house.

Mia Buchanan: Uh-huh. *winky face*

Yoshi Pennington: But I will say, I kind of like them.

I'm grinning so hard, my cheeks hurt.

My phone beeps with a new text. This one is from my father.

Dad: Any chance you can babysit Saturday night?

I read it quickly, but then return to texting Yoshi.

Mia Buchanan: Well, you are full of surprises.

As soon as I press SEND, I realize I sent *this* text to Dad. Oh my god. Oh my god.

I just sent the flirty text I'd meant for Yoshi to Dad!

Dad: What?

Yoshi Pennington: So we should probably talk about the festival. As much fun as this is.

Mia Buchanan: One sec. Dealing with an issue.

And then I switch screens. I am so dumb.

Mia Buchanan: I'm so sorry, Dad. I sent you the wrong text.

Dad: It's OK. You texting with Lark?

I bite my lip.

Mia: No, another friend.

Dad: Hang on, Lilou is crying. But Saturday night?

Yoshi Pennington: Everything OK?

Mia Buchanan: Sure. Saturday night sounds great.

Yoshi Pennington: Saturday night?

Mia Buchanan: Shoot. BRB.

Mia Buchanan: Sat night is good.

Dad: Great. Thanks, love. Say hi to your texting friend!

If my dad knew I was texting with a boy, how would he react? Dad is pretty easygoing. Shannon, too. Mom and Thierry are the ones who'd want to know more information. I return to the Yoshi text thread.

Mia Buchanan: I'm back now. Texting with too many people and getting confused.

Yoshi Pennington: Does this mean you have exciting plans for Saturday night?

I chuckle, but I'm feeling too flustered. Maybe it's time to wrap things up.

Mia Buchanan: Just babysitting. Anyway, I have to go down to dinner soon. Talk soon?

I hold my breath because it almost feels like he should be able to spot the lie. Though in truth, Mom is probably moments away from calling me down to eat.

Yoshi Pennington: Sure. Have a good night!

I put the phone next to me on the windowsill and then lean forward to rest my forehead on my knees. There was something so fun about texting with Yoshi. It was like I saw him as a totally different person. But it's also kind of nice to be alone right now, where I don't have to worry about being funny or flirty, and I can just relax.

And take the time to apologize to Lark for freaking out and running out of the library. I pick up my phone again.

> **Mia Buchanan:** So on a scale of one to one million, how much did I embarrass myself this afternoon?

It doesn't seem like Lark is on her phone, but sometimes it just takes her longer to get to it.

> **Mia Buchanan:** I'm really sorry I left without saying good-bye. Like more sorry than I was when I accidentally ate the chocolate cupcake in your lunch.

There's a long pause, and I wrap my arms around my knees.

> **Lark Mapp-Jefferson:** That wasn't an accident.

My stomach does a little, hopeful skip. But still, I tread carefully.

Mia Buchanan: I know. That was also crappy of me. I'm a terrible friend.

Lark Mapp-Jefferson: It's a good thing I have fond memories of you from when we were little.

I smile.

Mia Buchanan: So, Yoshi walked me home today . . .

Lark Mapp-Jefferson: And . . .

Mia Buchanan: And nothing. It was really fun.

There's a long pause where it once again seems like Lark isn't typing.

Mia Buchanan: OK. It was really, really fun. *swoons*

Lark Mapp-Jefferson: You know I'm going to say that you should tell him how you feel. So why even bring it up?

Mia Buchanan: All right, all right.

I pause, then type quickly.

Mia Buchanan: Any festival updates from your mom?

Lark Mapp-Jefferson: Nope. Gotta go. Talk later.

I feel unsettled, like things aren't in their proper places. Mom calls me down to dinner then, and I can barely pay attention to the food or conversation. Instead, I try to think of ways to save the festival, which is just about as unsuccessful as not thinking about the sudden awkwardness that was there between me and Lark.

Chapter Six

I wake up Saturday morning to a text from Lark.

Lark Mapp-Jefferson: Update from Mom: The town council meeting to discuss the festival will be held Sunday evening.

I debate how to respond and finally just send back a frowning face.

That means there's only thirty-six hours to come up with a plan. I should have spent less time texting with Yoshi last night and more time brainstorming.

I sit up in bed and bite my thumbnail. What if they

cancel the festival and everything that we've worked for is for nothing?

And I know it's silly, but I can't help thinking:

No sleigh ride.

No photograph to go in the series with Mom's, Grandma's, and Grandpa's.

And, of course, there's the new fear that we may have to sell the inn.

I sigh and check the weather apps on my phone. My heart leaps when I see something different: 80 percent chance of . . .

Wait.

Rain. Not snow. Rain.

Tonight.

My stomach sinks. Great.

I open the ten-day forecast and feel a beat of hope. Twenty percent chance of snow!

But that's only on the *last* day of the ten-day forecast, which is Monday. The day after the festival ends.

Too late and also not enough.

I toss my phone onto the big chair at the corner of my room where I like to do my homework and bury myself under my covers.

I feel like a bear: Wake me up when the weather is better.

Apparently, Mom doesn't think much of my becoming one with my inner bear. Half an hour later, I'm helping her with a weekend ritual: going through the inn to straighten up and making sure everything looks good.

News flash: It always looks good. Between the carefully preserved antique furniture to the tasteful decorations that Mom has been handpicking for decades, I feel like I live in a dollhouse.

But then I remember the conversation between Mom and Thierry in the kitchen, and I try to temper my irritation.

"I love this house." I sigh, perhaps a little too dramatically. "Especially at Christmas. It's so pretty with all the holly wreaths and the dark wood and . . ."

Mom frowns my way and then passes me a dusting rag. We have a cleaning staff, but they're working on preparing all the bedrooms upstairs, so Mom and I are doing the living room.

"It looks like it'll be a small crowd for dinner tonight," Mom says after a few moments of quiet. Well, outward quiet, since in my head I'm freaking out about the possibility of having to sell the inn. Must. Save. The. Inn.

"Mm-hmm." When we're not in our busy season, Thierry and Mom sit by the fire or on the back porch, enjoying a cup of tea in the evening. There's none of this stressful energy. The guests come and go, and the most pressing issue is when someone takes home one of our famous white plush bathrobes, or when Thierry can't decide between a warm soup and a cold soup. There's no tension. No raised voices.

"Thierry is making the chicken Provençal you like so much," Mom continues. "I know you're staying at your dad's tonight, but I thought you guys all might like to have dinner here."

"I think Dad and Shannon are going out tonight. They asked if I could babysit."

"Ah," Mom says, and she puts on the smile that is usually reserved for talking on the phone with guests at the inn. "Another time."

I nod, dusting an invisible spot on the coffee table.

"How are things at your dad's?" she asks.

"Good." I shrug.

I know I'm lucky when it comes to my parents. Mom married Thierry when I was three, and two years later, Dad married Shannon. Mom and Dad don't fight, but they also aren't best friends. They're almost like colleagues: cordial, committed to working together, and a little distant. They've been divorced since I was a baby, so I have no image in my mind of them being in love. I can't really even picture it, if I'm honest with myself. Dad is so laid-back, living out in the country, his hair a bit too long, his clothing a bit too threadbare. Apparently, when they were married, he'd helped my mom with the inn, which I can only imagine was a disaster. Dad's attention span for anything but his wood-working projects is . . . nonexistent. The number of times I've gone into his kitchen to find his forgotten vegetables on the cutting board and un-boiled water on the stove is more than I can easily recall.

"Lilou is getting a new tooth, so she's not really sleeping," I add. "And since she's sharing a room with Tabitha and Talulah . . ."

I glance up in time to see the tiniest hint of an eye roll from my mom. I giggle, because my mom almost never gives in to the urge to roll her eyes at Dad and Shannon's parenting style.

But she's right. Twin three-year-olds sharing a room with

a baby is a little much. Though, if it means I get my own room at Dad's, I won't argue. Better than sleeping in the den. Or on the couch.

"Well, give us a call if you need anything," Mom tells me, smoothing the bun at the nape of her neck. "We don't have that many guests to worry about," she adds, a little sadly.

I know, I think. I almost want to bring up what I overheard, but then the phone rings.

Mom winces.

"Do you want me to get it?" I ask, but she shakes her head and walks over to the desk.

"Good morning. This is the Rocking Horse Inn, Amy speaking."

Mom's putting up a brave front, but her shoulders are up near her ears.

And then I hear it: the dreaded words.

"Yes, unfortunately, we have no way of knowing whether it will snow for sure, but if you'd like to cancel . . ."

I turn away with a heavy sigh. I'm kind of glad I'm not sleeping here tonight.

"Are you sure you're all set?" Shannon asks me that evening as we stand in her living room, which is cluttered and colorful, a far cry from the inn. For all her laid-back, supercool attitude, Shannon can get anxious when it comes to leaving the littles. Even with me.

"I can have friends over for a party as long as the girls are watching TV, right?" I ask with a grin. This is our familiar routine. "And they need to be asleep by ten p.m.? With chocolates in hand?"

"Hardy har har." Shannon grimaces. She brings this on herself as far as I'm concerned. The girls love it when I babysit because I'm the only one who makes Snail's Pace Race into a competitive game instead of one of cooperation. And I bring treats.

It's pretty much my duty as a big sister. And another

reason I refuse to think about the possibility of moving. Not. Going. To. Happen.

"Thanks, sweetie." Dad puts one arm around me and kisses my temple. His beard is scratchy against my skin, but I wouldn't ask him to shave for anything. I found an old picture of him shaved once and . . . I think it scarred me.

"Call if you need anything," Shannon adds as Dad helps her into her ski jacket. "We're just going to Rachel and Andrew's house for dinner. They live up the mountain, but I'm sure they have reception up there." She bites the corner of her lip. I know that now she's wondering if that's true, what would happen if she was unreachable.

"Won't hesitate to call if anything comes up," I promise, holding up my phone. "And if for whatever reason you aren't reachable, Mom's home and she can help me."

Shannon nods, more to herself than to me. For the millionth time, I thank the gods that if there is any weirdness between Mom and Thierry and Dad and Shannon, they push it out of sight. While Shannon and Mom aren't besties, there's no question that Shannon would turn to Mom if she needed the help.

Reason number nine million why we can't leave Flurry.

I shove that thought away as Shannon finally shuts the door behind her. I turn to my sisters—my crazy, messy, and filthy sisters. Oy.

"Okay, so which one of you is Talulah and which is Tabitha?" I tease, hands on my hips.

"The baby is Tab," Tabitha informs me. She's trying to play it straight, but the tiniest grin threatens to take over her face and her blue eyes are shining. That's the only feature the four of us share: We all have Dad's deep blue eyes.

"Okay, Baby Tab," I say, picking up Talulah instead of Lilou. "Wait. Shouldn't you be sleeping in the crib by now?"

"Nooooo!" The twins screech with laughter. And Lilou, never one to miss an opportunity to be in on a joke, joins in with a giant burp.

I love my girls.

By the time I have them fed, bathed, and changed into pj's, I'm starting to wonder how any babysitter can do *anything* after taking care of three kids. I'd initially thought I could do some homework or watch TV, but I'm personally praying that I can get through their bedtime before I face-plant onto my own bed.

Luckily, Lilou is asleep in the sling I'm wearing, so apart from a backache and feeling like I'm attached to a pint-size furnace, I technically only have two kids to put to bed. Except, since it's Tully and Tab, it's the equivalent of fifteen kids.

"Books or stories?" I ask them as we plop onto the living room couch. I learned early on that you never offer to lie in one of their beds. They'll either fight about whose bed we get to lie in, or whose bed we *don't* lie in. Living room couch it is.

"Stories," Tabitha insists, and by some unprecedented miracle, Talulah agrees.

"Make-believe or real?" This time I turn to Talulah. She might have agreed with Tabitha's suggestion, but I'm not taking any risks of "it's not fair."

I really can't imagine why Shannon is worried about me babysitting. I know all the tricks already.

Talulah scrunches up her face and waits half a beat. "If she can't decide, can I say?" Tabitha interrupts.

"I know what I want," Talulah bellows.

Lilou stirs in my pouch, and I rock from side to side to make sure she's sleeping. I may have spoken too soon about my expertise.

Tabitha opens her mouth to argue.

Suddenly, there's a knock at the front door.

I glance at the kitchen clock. Eight. Definitely too early for Dad and Shannon to get back. Unless something happened . . .

I push off the couch as gracefully as I can, hoping that I can keep Lilou asleep.

"Mama says we shouldn't open the door for anyone," Tabitha cautions, her body so close behind mine that every time she steps, her toes graze my heels. Talulah, never one to be excluded from an adventure, is plastered to my thigh. One false step, and we'll land in a great big pile of arms and legs and a very unhappy Lilou.

"Who is it?" I call when I reach the door.

"Um, it's Yoshi? From next door?"

I freeze.

Yoshi? *My* Yoshi or another one . . .

I mean, not *my* Yoshi.

Agh!

I shift my gaze to the girls and they're grinning. "Hi, Yoshi!" Tabitha yells through the door, as though we've been locked inside the house for days, and he's found us. "My sister Mia is babysitting tonight!"

There's a beat of silence, and I wonder if Yoshi realizes it's *his* Mia. Shoot. Not that I'm *his* Mia but . . .

I'm blushing.

"Um, hi there, Ta . . ." Yoshi trails off, and I realize he's trying to figure out which kid just spoke to him.

With their very different hair lengths—Tab's is short and pixie-ish, and Tul's is long and curly—the girls are easy to tell apart. But I can't fault Yoshi for not being able to do so through the oak door. I can barely do it on the phone, and most of the time I'm just guessing.

"Girls, back up," I order, jiggling my body to keep Lilou from waking.

"But, Mia, we aren't supposed to open the door, unless there's a grown-up with us," Talulah says in a high whisper. I don't know who she thinks she's hiding from. I'm sure that Shannon and Dad can hear her from the top of whatever mountain they're on.

"Sweetie, I know Yoshi. And I'm technically the grown-up here."

"You aren't a grown-up," Tabitha says.

"It's fine, guys. You aren't opening the door by yourself. I'm here."

Except, now that I look down, I realize that in addition to carrying a sleeping—and drooling—Lilou, my sweatpants are totally stretched out, and I think there's a piece of orange macaroni stuck to my gray wool socks. Not that I should care what I look like in front of Yoshi. But it would be better if I didn't look like a total disaster. Never mind how I smell after wrestling the kids through dinner and bath time.

Whatever.

When I manage to jerk the door open, there's Yoshi on the porch, soaking wet. Soaking wet and shivering.

"Mia?" he says, frowning. "What are you doing here?"

"Babysitting my sisters." The outside air has turned colder, and it's only then that I realize it's not only raining, but it's freezing rain.

I can't believe that there's no snow, but we can have freezing rain. How is this fair?

"Wait, they're your sisters?" Yoshi asks, looking down at the littles with a surprised smile.

I realize that apart from our little texting conversation

last night, we've never really bridged that school-home divide.

"We have the same dad," I explain. "He married Shannon after he and my mom got divorced. Long time ago."

"Oh, okay." He nods. "Small world."

I glance over to the twins in their mismatched pajama tops and bottoms, their sleep diapers peeking out the top. "Seriously. I didn't know you knew the littles."

"The littles?"

I chuckle. "That's what I call them. Right, littles?" I turn down to face them, and they erupt in giggles.

"Ah." He nods. He keeps wiggling his nose like he's about to sneeze, and his whole face is soaking.

Shoot. I shouldn't be leaving him on the porch. "Uh, do you want to come in?" I ask uncertainly.

He nods, shivering. "Thanks, that would be great."

"Sorry," I say as he steps inside. "I should have asked right away." I close the door behind him and mutter to myself, "I'm an idiot."

"Idiot! Idiot!" Tabitha shrieks. And then Talulah joins in, and my two adorable sisters are dancing around the living room screaming the word *idiot*.

I have a friend over. He's a boy. The kids are not asleep. And, apparently, I've just given them permission to use the word *idiot*. I'm so never getting to babysit again.

"Girls, I didn't say that word. I said . . ." What sounds like *idiot*? Shoot. Shoot. I stare at Yoshi, pleading with him to figure something out.

"She said *idiom*!" he jumps in, and I raise my eyebrows at him. *Idiom?* "It means an expression," he says, shrugging.

Which makes no sense at all, and yet, at least now the twins are dancing around screaming *idiom*.

Except now Lilou is awake. Shoot.

"Talulah, can you please get Yoshi a towel to dry off?" I ask. "Tabitha, do you know where Daddy's big sweatshirts are?"

Tabitha shakes her head, her eyes wide, as though she has no idea what any of those words mean. Meanwhile, Talulah has grabbed Yoshi a . . . dishcloth from the kitchen. Sigh.

"Yoshi, the bathroom is just down the hall," I say. "I think it would be easier if you just grabbed a towel yourself."

I only realize I'm doing the bobbing-up-and-down dance when Yoshi stares at me like I'm a creature from an alien planet.

I'm not a creature from an alien planet. I'm a big sister/ babysitter who has three awake charges, the boy she maybe has a crush on right in front of her, and no peace in sight.

This is not good.

Chapter Seven

Finally, I put on a TV show for Talulah and Tab (bad baby-sitter) and whisper through the bathroom door to Yoshi, my friend-who-is-a-boy-who's-over-while-my-parental-units-aren't-home (bad babysitter), that I'm going to try to get Lilou to sleep. And then I try to calm my racing heart as I settle into the rocking chair in the girls' room with Lilou.

The trick with rocking Lilou to sleep is pretending you don't care either way. You just happen to be sitting there, just happen to be holding her little body close to yours, just happen to be moving back and forth. It still takes her a while to stop straining toward the door and listening to figure out what might be happening out there. But after a few minutes, her breaths have evened out and she's making that sucking sound with her mouth like she's dreaming of milk.

I love Lilou. She still has that delicious baby smell. I snuggle her close, then put her into her crib.

When I make it out to the living room, I'm so calm I feel almost blissed out. Which is why I barely react when I see that my sisters have abandoned the show I put on for them. They're now perched on either side of Yoshi on the couch as he reads them a story.

I've never seen my sisters pass up a TV show for anything. Except maybe presents on their birthday.

If they notice me take a seat on the armchair beside them, they don't give me a sign. I curl up on the chair, pulling the scratchy afghan on top of my knees, and listen to the old Greek myth that Yoshi is reading from my dad's mammoth collection, the one he used to read to me when I was little. Yoshi's voice is so deep, so calm, that even I am lulled half to sleep as he spins tales of gods gone rogue, turning on one another and the humans who live in their time.

I don't know how much my sisters understand, but there's something about the tone of his voice, the lilting quality of his speech, that makes it mesmerizing.

And before I know it, he's closing the book and I realize that the girls are sleeping. Each of them leaning against either side of Yoshi, pinning him in place. When he catches my eye, he smiles wryly, and my cheeks flush. Because if I didn't notice the story ending, the girls falling asleep, clearly I also . . .

I really hope I didn't drool.

"I can try to move them," I say, my voice cracking from lack of use. I definitely fell asleep. Shoot. Shoot. Shoot.

"That seems like tempting fate," he says quietly.

We sit in the quiet living room, sleeping littles around us. I glance over at Yoshi and he sends me a tiny smile, like he's both smiling and not smiling at the same time.

"Why are you here?" I ask him.

His eyebrows go up. I'm such an *idiom*.

"I didn't mean it like that," I try again. "I'm glad you're here. I mean, I'm glad—"

I have no idea what I'm glad about. Right now, probably just that he isn't laughing hysterically at me.

"Sorry. I meant, why did you come to the door before? Were you looking for my dad or Shannon? Because they aren't here."

Thanks for that, Captain Obvious, I think.

"I got locked out of my house," Yoshi explains with a sigh. "My folks are stuck up in Kildare for the night. The streets are too icy to risk them coming back here right now. And your dad and Shannon said that if I ever had a problem, I could . . ." He shrugs.

"Of course," I say. "Of course."

Of course. Not a problem at all. Yoshiki Pennington is sitting in Dad's living room.

We are alone here. No problem at all. Because we're just friends. It's like being here with Lark.

The lights flicker, and we immediately look at each other. No. No. No. No.

"Do you have candles and flashlights?" Yoshi asks.

Thankfully, yes. "My dad has an extensive collection. He's pretty well prepared for things like this."

Paying for college, not so much. But blackouts are no big deal.

The lights flicker again. If I'd been alone, I'm quite sure that I would have panicked and prayed that Dad and Shannon were close to home. But having Yoshi here makes me feel braver. We spring into action. We get a pile of candles and matches, flashlights and extra batteries, and warm blankets for the girls. I check on Lilou, who is sleeping soundly in her crib, and cover her with a fuzzy blanket. I come back out to the living room to see that Yoshi has even dug up the wind-up radio I remember using as a toy when I was little. It still works.

When the lights do go out, it isn't as much of a shock. We cover the twins with the blankets, and they remain sleeping on either side of Yoshi as he sits down between them again. I huddle back under the blanket on the chair.

"Are you okay?" Yoshi asks when we're all settled in.

I sweep the room with my eyes. The candles keep the darkness at bay, but they also provide a lovely glow. It's almost like you can't see all the mess, the disorder, in the dark. Everything is muted.

"I don't know what I would have done if you hadn't shown up," I say. It's both an answer and not an answer, and he doesn't seem bothered by that.

"I'm sure you would have figured everything out. But I can imagine it's nice to have an extra pair of hands."

I want to tell him that he's been much more than an extra pair of hands, but I don't know how to string all those words together so that they come out well.

"You probably wish you were in your warm house, where you don't have to have the littles draped all over you," I say instead, trying to insert chuckles at the appropriate moments.

"I don't," he says. I can't quite see his expression in the candlelight, but I hear the truth in his words.

"What's it like to be an only child?" I ask before I think better of it. Mom always says that you need to be careful with personal questions because you never know what they'll unearth. I've heard her talk about what it's like to be the host of an inn, where your job is to be friendly and polite, but where you need to dodge the landmines you might not even realize are there.

Yoshi shrugs. "I've never known anything different. I have no idea what it's really like to have siblings. I guess there are some things that are good about being an only child and some things that aren't great. I never have to fight with anyone about what game to play or what movie to watch or who has to clear the table. But, if my parents aren't in the mood for a game or a movie, there's nobody to hang out with me. What's it like having so many siblings?"

I think hard instead of just giving him a pat answer. "It's weird," I finally admit. "On the one hand, I have my sisters.

But I don't live with the girls full-time, so it's different. And plus, we might have the same crazy dad, but Shannon and my mom are so different. Even though the girls are so small, they're already as different from me as Lark is. And then on top of that, I'm an only child when I'm at Mom's house. And in some ways, I *feel* like an only child because there's nobody else who has my kooky, laid-back dad and my uptight, proper mom. And who has Thierry as this brilliant chef stepdad and Shannon as a hippie stepmom. I'm this odd combination of all these people but . . ."

I feel like I'm babbling. I've never said these words out loud, and I'm not even sure that I ever knew I thought them. There's something about Yoshi and the darkness and quiet and the sleeping littles that makes the whole scene feel surreal. And simple.

"I get that," he says. "I think everyone feels a little out of place sometimes. But maybe for people like us, without siblings in a conventional way, it's a lot more intense." He chuckles. "Though I have the added bonus of being the only person with a Japanese mom and British dad, who grew up in Southern California and got uprooted to move literally across the country."

There's a strain in his voice, and I try to think back to the reason I heard for why Yoshi and his parents moved here. But I can't remember.

"Did your parents move here for a job?"

He nods, a motion so small that it almost seems like it didn't happen. "My mom is a pediatrician. And apparently there's only one other in town?"

"Right, because Dr. Pine retired last year." Dr. Pine was a great doctor, not one of those who told you no candy and no screens. "Mom loved her because she was no-nonsense. She believed in moderation, and that most things could be cured by more exercise, more sleep, and healthier food. But she wasn't fanatical about it."

Yoshi laughs so quietly I almost miss it. "Not sure how she'll feel about my mom, then. She's a big believer that everything can be solved by cutting out sugar and wheat."

"No!" I shudder. I'm glad we've already switched to Dr. Zwiebel.

"However, she's won all sorts of awards for her research and for some of the programs she's developed to fight childhood obesity."

I want to ask him what he's allowed to eat at home, but it seems a little too personal. Even though we're sitting in the dark, surrounded by the littles, in my dad's house.

It's crazy.

"Your dad does the weather on WVVW, right?" I ask. I've seen Mr. Pennington, handsome and dapper, on our local news station.

There's a long pause, and Yoshi's voice is quieter when he answers. "Yup. He's a meteorologist. When we lived in San Diego, he worked at a big TV station."

I feel like I'm missing something, that his tone and his words don't match.

"Does he miss the station in San Diego?" I ask.

"No. Definitely not." This time, his words are a little

more forceful. "WVVW is a much better fit. He gets to report on the weather without all the . . ." He pauses, and I don't interrupt the silence. "Without all the politics."

His words sound practiced, almost like a script or something he's heard so many times that he's repeating it. But I don't know where the landmines are, so I don't ask any more questions.

I focus on the sound of the ice falling against the windows. Too bad it's not snow.

"What do we do if the power doesn't come on soon?" Yoshi asks before I can think of how to respond to his statement about his dad.

"Have you never been in an ice storm?" I ask.

He shakes his head. His eyes are focused on the kitchen window where tiny pings of ice are hitting the glass. It's odd to think that he's probably also never been in a snowstorm.

"Well, we have a ton of firewood, so we won't get too cold. This isn't that unusual. I mean, it sucks that it's nighttime, but at least we don't have to figure out how to entertain the kids without screens. And my dad's car has four-wheel drive, so as soon as it's safe enough, he and Shannon will be home."

"Do you know how to make a fire?"

I nod. "I mean, I'd rather if my dad did it. I think he would, too. But if I needed to? Absolutely. Everyone in Flurry knows how to."

The wind howls outside, but it's a familiar sound. This is just winter in Vermont.

"Will you teach me one day?" Yoshi asks.

"To make a fire?"

He nods.

"Sure. Or maybe my dad can teach you. He's the expert. Unless your dad—"

"He doesn't know how." The words are sharp. I don't know how to reply, but luckily, it seems like Yoshi isn't waiting for me to, because he continues. "It feels so dumb. We're here in this small town in Vermont that is known for being super outdoorsy, and we can't do any of that stuff. We all swim, and we surf and barbecue. In California, we're just like everyone else. But here in Flurry? My parents don't know how to build a fire. We don't snowboard or ski or skate or . . ."

His voice has trailed off, like he's run out of steam.

"I could teach you all that," I say slowly. I'm not sure it's the right thing to say, if that's what Yoshi would want. Maybe he's just looking for someone to understand why he feels like a fish out of water. Maybe he wants to go back to California or . . .

"I'd like that," he whispers, and my heart aches. Because I'm in such trouble. I've had crushes before, but nothing has been like this. They've been fleeting, and on boys who often didn't even know I existed. It's easy to have a crush on someone who can't possibly return your feelings.

But Yoshi? What happens when you have a crush on someone who's a friend? Do you risk the friendship on the possibility he feels the same way? Or do you tell yourself that friendships last much longer than crushes do?

I have no answers. So we sit still and listen to the wind and the icy rain, with the candles flickering all around us.

Dad and Shannon make it home before the house even starts to get cold. This house is so well insulated (thanks, Dad!) that we were probably good for a few more hours at least.

While it was really nice just hanging out with Yoshi, I'm relieved to see Dad and Shannon come through the door.

"Yoshi!" Dad says, sounding pleasantly surprised. "What happened?"

Yoshi explains how he was locked out and his parents are away for the night. He also explains that he and I know each other from school.

Shannon gives me a small eyebrow raise and a half smile, as if she senses something, and I try not to blush. But I also know that she sees us surrounded by the sleeping littles and realizes that everything has been totally innocent.

But even just *thinking* that makes me blush more.

Dad builds a small fire in the fireplace while Shannon carries the littles to their beds. Then Dad makes up the couch for Yoshi to sleep on. I say good night to everyone and head to my room. I can't stop thinking about the fact that there's a boy—a boy I like—sleeping in my living room. A boy who brushed his teeth in the bathroom I use. And yes, there are two grown-ups and three littles in the house with us but . . .

There's something about the whole thing that gives me goose bumps. Because I'm not sure I really have a choice about my feelings for Yoshi anymore.

I climb into bed and pull the covers up. It isn't until I'm almost asleep that I realize that in all the time Yoshi and I spent talking and hanging out tonight, we never even discussed the festival. I barely even thought about it.

And the town council meeting is tomorrow.

Chapter Eight

I have never had so much trouble eating breakfast as I do this morning with Yoshi at Dad's house.

I mean, seriously? Who knew I had to concentrate on getting the fork to my mouth? Usually, it just gets there on its own. But today, it hits every spot except the appropriate destination. Same with the cup of orange juice. Thankfully, the power is back on, so at least *something* feels normal.

"So, I was thinking about the festival when I was trying to fall asleep," Yoshi starts as we clear the table. I trip over the area rug that's been in the kitchen ever since I can remember. Luckily, I don't drop anything. I can't think of Yoshi trying to fall asleep on my couch. It's just too . . . weird.

"Uh-huh," I say, trying for noncommittal.

"I know the town council is going to make whatever decision they are going to make. But I was serious when I told you I'd help you with planning an alternate solution."

"That would be great," I say. "Maybe we can work on it today? I mean, since the meeting is tonight and . . ."

Wait. Is this kind of like asking him out? On a date?

"I mean, whatever." I start to ramble. "Totally fine if you can't. I can also . . ." Someone please stop me. Where are my ever-present sisters when I actually need them to interrupt? Why do I suddenly wish I could take out my phone so Yoshi and I could text back and forth instead of talking?

"Let's do it!" Yoshi's voice is full of excitement, and I feel a bit better. Except I'm still not sure if he's just excited to plan for the festival, or to spend more time with me. I wish I could text Lark to ask her advice. I guess I'll see her tonight at the council meeting.

"Yoshi," Dad says, coming into the kitchen with his phone. "I just talked to your parents and they're still not back in Flurry. You're totally welcome to stay here until they return."

Yoshi straightens his back as Dad talks to him, and then he nods. "Are you sure it's okay?" Yoshi asks. "Mia and I were going to do some work together . . ."

Dad's eyes flash to mine and I'm reminded of the text I accidentally sent him the other day. I smile, trying to assume a placid look. "Festival stuff," I confirm.

"Sounds good," Dad says. "I'm going to go around the area to see if anyone needs help. But Shannon and the girls will be in and out. Why don't you guys work in the living room? I can build you a nice fire if you'd like."

And Shannon and the girls will be able to keep an eye on you, he seems to be silently saying.

"Sounds good!" I echo back with a cheery smile.

Yoshi and I grab a bowl of clementines and some napkins and get settled on the couch in the living room.

"Here's my question: Has there ever been a snowless fes-tival?" Yoshi asks.

I know that in order to brainstorm for this possibility, we need to call it what it is—*snowless*—but it still hurts my stomach. "Not as far as I know." I start peeling the clemen-tines just so I have something to do with my hands. "We have pictures of the festival up at the inn from a bunch of different years. Some even pretty old. But there's never been one without snow."

I think about the photographs I walk past every day. I love seeing how they go from black-and-white photos with everyone dressed up fancy, to color pictures but still nice outfits, to color pictures with jeans and jackets that appar-ently made my grandma *tsk*.

In all of the pictures, there are enormous snowdrifts and people in snowshoes and skis.

"There was one year where I think the temperature was way warmer than expected in December," I remember out loud. That year we had snow on the ground already, and it felt odd to be walking around with open ski jackets and no hats and gloves. I was really young then, and one of my biggest memories was that everything was wet. "It wasn't a great year for the festival. Too many of the events didn't work all that well because things melted."

"What about other years when the weather didn't cooperate?" Yoshi asks.

I think back, festival by festival. "I know one year there was a snowstorm in the middle of the festival, so certain events were moved indoors. Apparently, that was also kind of disastrous, and it took a few years for the festival to bounce back."

"Hmm," Yoshi says. "It's a shame, because one of my ideas was that we could move the festival indoors."

"But how? The festival is all about snow."

"I hadn't really figured that part out yet," Yoshi admits. "I'm just trying to think of what we do in SoCal when the weather isn't good and we're supposed to have a surf competition or an outdoor event. Sometimes you can move it inside. Other times you postpone it. Sometimes you change the venue—"

Change the venue.

"Wait."

Change the venue!

"What if we . . ." I trail off as I start listing the events in my head. Some we could move inside. For others, we could change the venue. For some, we could change the activity.

"Um, you're not talking and I can't read your mind," Yoshi says, and I nod quickly. But I can't lose this train of thought. "Talk and I'll take notes." He grabs a pad of paper and pencil from the coffee table.

"Okay, humor me," I say. "Let's make a list of everything that happens at the festival. Maybe what we should be thinking of is not one solution for the entire festival, but multiple solutions."

Yoshi nods, and together we map out the festival as it currently exists by category.

Events
Cross-Country Ski Marathon
Snowshoe Races
World's Biggest Snowball Fight

Building
Sled Building
Snowman Building
Competitive Igloo Making

Art & Food
Craft fair
Ice sculptures
Food trucks

"Let's take out the ones that don't require snow," Yoshi

suggests, and I nod. We don't need to worry about the craft

fair or the food trucks.

"But then there's other stuff," I point out. "Like ice

skating, ice fishing, cross-country ski trails, snowshoeing trails, and downhill skiing at the Top of the Mountain Ski Chalet . . ."

"Assuming the weather stays as it is, are we fine with those?" Yoshi asks.

I think it over. "The only ones that would be a problem are the ski and snowshoeing trails here in town. Top of the Mountain makes their own snow. And they probably have *some* snow a little higher up."

Yoshi chews on the tip of the pencil. Then he must realize what he's doing, because he takes it out of his mouth and smiles meekly. "Bad habit," he says.

I shrug. There are plenty of pencils. "Okay, let's rearrange the list into categories of what kinds of solutions they need. Like the ones that don't require snow can be held indoors or outdoors, even if there's no snow."

"Sled Building probably doesn't need snow," Yoshi says.

I shake my head. "They have a race at the end."

"Okay," he says slowly. "Maybe we need to also think about which events can be changed."

"You're right," I allow.

"Really?" he asks and then winks.

Yoshiki Pennington just winked at me. I have to keep my squeeing on the inside.

We break for lunch and eat the warmed-up vegetable stew that Shannon serves. Still, we can't stop talking about the festival, even at the table. I've taken notes and we've now figured out solutions for a bunch of the events.

<u>Events that we don't need to worry about</u>
Skating—outdoors, no snow required
Ice fishing—outdoors, no snow required .
Downhill skiing—snow at the mountain already
Craft fair—no snow required

Food trucks—outdoors, no snow required

Ice sculptures—outdoors, no snow required

Sled Building—can be done indoors or outside without snow, but race?

<u>Snow-dependent events</u>

Cross-Country Ski Marathon—can it be done at Top of the Mountain? Would need new course.

Snowshoe Races—can it be done at Top of the Mountain? Would need new course.

Biggest Snowball Fight—must have snow

Snowman Building—must have snow

Igloo Making—must have snow, but could we bring snow from the mountain or the snow makers and have people assemble igloos from bricks we've already dug out?

While it's not hard to change snowshoeing to hiking if there's no snow, a lot of the regular kid-friendly snow activities are hard to move indoors. Which means that a lot of the activities that are great for kids would have to be canceled.

We finish lunch and go back to the living room to keep

working. By the early afternoon, Talulah and Tab start to bounce off the walls from the lack of physical activity and too much time together.

"Any chance you guys want to babysit them?" Shannon asks me and Yoshi, trying to get the girls to settle down.

I frown, feeling guilty. "Um . . . it's just that we don't have much time left before Yoshi's parents come home and then the council meeting. But maybe . . ."

She waves her hand. "I was mostly joking. But here's my advice: No matter what you remove from the festival, if you put in a day camp that will take care of kids while adults do fun things? Nobody will get mad at you for anything!"

A day camp for kids . . .

Yoshi and I turn to each other, both of our mouths open.

"Snow Carnival!" we both say at the same time.

"But wait." Yoshi frowns. "Doesn't the Snow Carnival need snow?"

"Well, yes," I allow. "But . . ." I think through the events we'd proposed, back when we'd first come up with the carnival in September. They were all basically carnival games with a snow theme. "I actually think all the events can be done without snow."

Yoshi squints as he goes through the list in his head, but I get impatient.

"Snowball toss, snowball bowling, snowball bull's-eye, snowball golf, snowball volleyball, tic-tac-snow, frozen bubble blowing, snow graffiti, and the snow obstacle course." I count them off on my fingers. Nine. Nine amazing events that we'd totally figured out and then had to shelve. And now . . .

"We can bring back the Snow Carnival!" I say with glee.

"We totally can," Yoshi says, and his eyes are sparkling.

Later, Yoshi's parents come home, so he can return to his house. Then Dad drives me back to the inn.

There, I go up to my room and open my laptop to keep working. Yoshi and I text back and forth, the ideas still coming fast and furious.

Yoshi Pennington: I found the plans for the carnival we drew up in student council. Looks like all the booths can be done indoors or outdoors.

Mia Buchanan: Looking at the same plans . . .

Yoshi Pennington: YES! *fist bump*

Mia Buchanan: *fist bump* back

Yoshi Pennington: Another event that we could suggest adding—apart from the snow carnival—is rock climbing. Because you said Lark and her dad go somewhere nearby?

Mia Buchanan: OMG. Lark and Chris would love that.

Yoshi Pennington: This is going to be seriously cool.

I bite my lip, staring at my phone. He's right, it's a really good plan. But how do we get the town council to hear it before they make their decision?

Mia Buchanan: Maybe we should go to Lark's house and talk to her mom about all this. That way she'll have something to bring to the council?

It takes me a few extra seconds before I press SEND. I'm not sure it's a great idea. I don't want to put more pressure on Soleil.

Yoshi Pennington: How much time do we have?

I glance down at my phone. Shoot. It's almost three and the meeting is at seven.

Mia Buchanan: Not that much. Want to meet there in an hour?

Yoshi Pennington: *smiley face*

And I grin so hard, I'm almost not nervous.

"Long time no see," I say as I meet Yoshi in front of Lark's house.

His smile is more like a smirk, and maybe I'm slaphappy from doing all this planning or not sleeping well last night (YOSHI PENNINGTON WAS IN MY DAD'S HOUSE SLEEPING IN THE LIVING ROOM!!!!!), but I smirk right back at him. And then giggle.

I'm a dolt.

"Ready?" Yoshi says, holding out his hand.

Lark is going to freak out if she sees us holding hands. Even though we're not really holding hands. He just held out his hand. Totally different. But still . . .

I put my hand in his, his palm smooth and cool while I think mine is a little warm and sweaty. We kind of shake on it, then pull our hands back.

Um, awkward?

I quickly knock on Lark's door. I'd texted her before, explaining that Yoshi and I had ideas for the festival, and she'd said it was fine for us to come over. But I hadn't told her that Yoshi and I had hung out last night. That's for later.

"Hey, guys!" Soleil says as she opens the door.

She ushers us in and we step inside. Lark is sitting in the living room, playing a game on her phone. When she sees me and Yoshi, she smiles and waves, but I can feel a slight distance in her manner. Why? This is so weird.

Soleil claps her hands. "I hear you guys have a proposal for me."

While her smile is bright, the dark circles under her eyes

are more prominent, and the concealer she dabbed on is clearly not doing an adequate job covering them up. I want to tell her it's no problem, that actually, we don't want to rock the boat. But then I remember the inn and the possibility that Mom may have to sell it. And I forge ahead.

"We hope you like it," I say instead. "We know you guys will do what's best for the town, and we just wanted to help out."

I can feel Yoshi's presence beside me, and I wonder if he's going to interrupt, take over, since I seem to be failing at sounding convincing. But he remains silent, and I'm grateful for that.

"Thanks, hon," Soleil says, pulling me into a familiar hug. "Now, tell me all about your idea."

Chapter Nine

The wait outside the council meeting is almost enough to drive me crazy. Lark, Yoshi, Kyle, Marcus, and I sit on chairs in the drafty corridor of our town hall building. On the other side of the big wooden door, the council is talking.

I wring my hands. Despite all the ideas that we've generated and all the planning we've already done . . . they could still say no. They could still decide to cancel everything.

Plus, Marcus isn't speaking to me because he's annoyed that he wasn't part of the planning meetings Yoshi and I had. I told him that it wasn't a big deal, that it was just the two of us talking, that Lark and Kyle weren't there, either, but he was unmoved.

And Lark is still being kind of cold.

Which is just what I need.

"Stop biting your nails," Lark says, and I drop my hand. Just like the other six times she mentioned it. We've made a deal that we won't talk about the festival until we hear their decision, but for the life of me, I can't find anything else to talk about.

They're deciding on the fate of the festival as we sit here. My mom's in there. Maayan is in there. But I'm stuck out here.

I pull out my phone.

Mia Buchanan: This is so painful.

I don't glance up. I don't move.

Yoshi Pennington: TOTALLY.

Mia Buchanan: Stop shouting, they're going to hear you inside and know we're out here.

A slight scoffing sound comes from Yoshi's direction. I stare at my phone, trying not to laugh.

> **Yoshi Pennington:** You're right. I'm sorry. *shrugs*
>
> **Mia Buchanan:** Tell me a story.
>
> **Yoshi Pennington:** Like a fairy tale?

I start to shake my head and then freeze. Everything needs to be communicated in text.

> **Mia Buchanan:** No. Tell me a real story. Tell me something that most people don't know.

I don't dare glance up. I stare at the phone in my hands instead. Finally, I see the dots signaling that he's typing, and I let the air trapped in my lungs out. Slowly.

> **Yoshi Pennington:** Hmmm. OK. I think I have something.

I wait and my breathing goes shallow for a long moment. Everything else seems to disappear: the council meeting, Marcus, Lark, and Kyle sitting around us.

> **Mia Buchanan:** Tell me.

It's like, even though we're in public and with other people, we aren't. We're alone.

Yoshi Pennington: When my parents announced we were moving, I was furious. I didn't want to come here. I tried to convince them that I could live with my best friend, Paz.

Mia Buchanan: I get that more than you know. Do you still feel that way?

Yoshi Pennington: Not really. I was really worried that it would be hard to make friends because people here would be so different. But truthfully, now the only thing I'm kind of scared of is the snow coming. Which I know is the opposite of how I should be feeling. Given the festival and all. But the thing is, I'm used to being good at outdoorsy things and . . . I don't know how to skate or how to ski. I'm worried that I won't be able to do the stuff you guys have been doing since you were babies. It's hard being an outsider. I feel like I finally fit in, but . . . I'm scared that will change.

I want to turn and face him. I want to walk over to where he's sitting, a couple of seats down, and move his bag off the chair beside him and tell him that it will be okay. But I can't. This game we're playing has rules, even if they're unspoken.

"Mia," Lark says, tugging my arm. "Maayan just said we should come inside."

For a long moment, I have no idea what she's talking about, and then I remember the council meeting and the festival. I can't believe I was so wrapped up in texting Yoshi that I didn't notice Maayan peeking her head out the door.

But strangely, I wish the council could continue without us for another few minutes, maybe an hour even, so I could keep texting with Yoshi. I want to make sure he knows he's part of our circle, and we won't let him feel like an outsider.

Lark and the others stand up, gathering their things.

"Give me a sec," I say to Lark. "I just need to . . ."

I press SEND and wait to see the typing dots. I should turn my head and see if he's even still sitting there, if he's walking toward the doors. But I can't. I can only stare at the small screen and hope . . .

Yoshi Pennington: Thank you. *smiley face*

I don't even try to hide the massive grin that's taken over my face. Shoving my phone into my pocket, I turn to Lark.

"For someone who is so invested in the festival, you really don't seem to care that much what the decision is," Lark says, and I startle at the anger in her voice.

"I care." I know I'm acting defensive, but I feel like I'm under attack.

"Well, then, stop flirting with Yoshi and let's get this over with."

I flinch. This is a different Lark than the one I know so well. Sure, she's often anxious these days because of the stress on her mom, but this feels like something else. She's a few steps in front of me before I find my voice. "How did you even know—"

She turns and treats me to an eye roll. "First, it was totally obvious just by looking at you guys. And second? It was just as hard to get Yoshi's attention as yours. You guys were glued to whatever was happening on your phones."

"I . . . um . . ," It's hard to even form words right now. How can I describe what's going on?

"Whatever. You'll tell me when you need me." And then she walks more quickly than I've ever seen her walk, just to get away from me.

I follow behind, swallowing hard.

There are twelve people on the city council, plus Soleil, but the noise they make could rival our cafeteria on a good day.

"Is it always like this?" I whisper to Lark before I remember what just happened in the corridor. She shrugs. Her eyes are fixed on her mom sitting at the end of the table, her back rounded in exhaustion. Miss Marks from the bank and Mr. Han, my old dance teacher, are both standing in front of her and they're practically shouting.

On the other side of the room, Maayan is being harangued by Bari from the bakery.

I find my mom on the left side of the table and she gives me a small smile, but apart from that little positive facial movement, I'm not getting any vibes from anyone else around the table. Mostly since they don't seem to be paying attention to us.

I'm glad I opted to wear my brown corduroy skirt and teal sweater because at least I look presentable.

When Soleil finally sees us, she puts on a broad smile. But I don't think it's fooling anyone. She motions for us to sit on the outskirts of the table and then bangs her gavel on a pad. It takes a few times before everyone stops talking.

"As I mentioned before the break," Soleil says when every-one is seated, "I wanted to invite the seventh-grade student council into the final part of the meeting since they've also been working so hard on the festival. They came to me this afternoon with plans that made it clear they're every bit as concerned with the fate of the festival as we are, and are invested in finding a solution. I'm sure you all know Mia Buchanan, Marcus Andelman, Yoshiki Pennington, Kyle Jones, and my daughter, Lark Mapp-Jefferson."

There's a smattering of applause. I shift uncomfortably in my seat, feeling nervous.

Soleil turns to us. "First, I wanted to let you all know where we're at in our discussions." She pauses, and there's tension in the air. Several people are staring down, and others have their arms crossed in front of them.

Tough crowd.

"The council has voted not to cancel the festival."

I want to whoop and cheer, but that's clearly not the right reaction, considering that most people in the room appear unhappy.

"The council felt that we're too close to the festival,

timewise, and that many people would be arriving whether we keep the festival or not," Soleil continues. "We determined that it would have a negative impact if visitors got here and found that there was nothing going on."

Okay, it's not a raging declaration of faith, but I'll take it.

She turns back to the council. "As I mentioned to some of you, these seventh graders presented me with a plan for saving the festival that was very similar to the one Anaya Sodhi gave on behalf of the festival committee." Soleil nods to Anaya, the lady who owns the town's best clothing boutique. "Just so you guys know," Soleil says, turning back to us, "we've decided to put in place a number of those ideas. The ice skating, ice fishing, and ice sculpture competition can all remain, as they don't depend on snow. The same goes for the food trucks and snack stands, of course. We will be moving the sled building to the civic center, and the craft fair will remain in the Hopkins Mansion."

I sneak a glance at Yoshi, but I can't read his face. I think this is all good news, but who can be sure?

"We're canceling snowshoeing and replacing it with some hiking options. Your suggestion of offering rock climbing was an interesting one, but apparently it's too cold for regular rock climbing and there isn't enough ice for ice climbing." Soleil gives Lark a small frown, and Lark nods understandingly. "We've discussed moving the cross-country skiing to the Top of the Mountain, since they make their own snow. That will likely happen, which will be great."

I clench my stomach muscles. I feel like there's a *but* coming.

"Unfortunately, some of our favorite activities will have to be canceled unless we miraculously see a huge snowfall." This time Soleil is staring into the middle of the table, like she's not happy making eye contact with anyone. "We have no way of replacing the Igloo Making competition or the final town-wide snowball fight. We're not even sure that we can do the cross-country skiing marathon. And, two things that will affect these students the most: We won't be able to have Snowman Building. And we won't be able to have the customary sleigh ride for the junior festival coordinator."

My stomach sinks. I know I should be grateful that we're having the festival at all. That's what's ultimately important. But we were so excited for the Snowman Building.

And if there's no sleigh ride, how will I get the picture that will match the ones of Mom, Grandma, and Grandpa?

My eyes fill with tears, and I dig my nails into my palms. I almost reach for Lark, but then I don't.

Soleil looks at me, Marcus, Kyle, Lark, and Yoshi. "The town council is well aware of how much work you all have put into the Snowman Building, and we're hoping that work will make it easier for whoever is running the event next year."

No event for us to run. No sleigh ride. It's pretty much a disaster.

"What about the Snow Carnival?" I interrupt, springing to my feet. It's only after the words are out of my mouth that I realize that as yet, nobody has interrupted Soleil, which probably means it's against the rules. Oops.

Soleil gives me a sad smile. "We discussed the Snow Carnival idea," she says slowly. "The council felt that there was too little time to properly plan—"

"But we can do it," I interrupt again. There are murmurings of disapproval, but this is too important to risk losing. "We wrote up very extensive plans back in September, including diagrams and drawings."

"But your plan involved the presence of snow," Soleil points out.

Right. I'm about to sit down when Yoshi gets up out of his seat to stand beside me.

"Is it okay to jump in?" Yoshi says. Soleil and I nod. "Mia and I have gone through all the plans that the student council created and they can *all* actually work without snow. It's just a matter of painting the different booths—"

"But we haven't even approved the Snow Carnival booths. What if they're not appropriate or safe?" Mr. Han demands.

I used to love Mr. Han as a dance teacher, but right now he's at the bottom of my list of people I like.

"We can bring them to Mayor Mapp-Jefferson to review tonight," I suggest, looking hopefully at Soleil.

Soleil shakes her head. "I'm afraid there's too much to do with the festival changing this year. I can't afford to take more time out to work with you guys."

I know that she's right, but I can't believe Soleil would say that. I thought she loved talking with us about all our ideas.

"Can't Maayan be our go-between?" Yoshi asks, nodding at our supervisor. "She's been working with us all this time. She knows we're dedicated and that we're committed to succeeding. Maybe she can be in touch with someone on the council to make sure there's nothing that could go wrong."

"I don't know . . ." Soleil says, turning to the council.

I feel like everything is slipping through our fingers, so I take one last chance. It's probably a long shot but . . .

"The Snow Carnival isn't just important because it gives us something to contribute," I explain, trying to keep the nervousness out of my voice. "Or because it's the perfect activity for little kids to do at the festival. It's important because it's all about snow. If we are going to essentially have a snowless Flurry Winter Festival, then we need to find a way to *still* bring snow into it. There can be snowball tosses and snowball golf and snowball bowling. We can use giant cotton balls, for instance. So we'll have snow there in some form. Does that make sense?"

I turn to the council and I see confused looks on their faces. Shoot. It didn't work. I'm about to sit down, defeated, when Yoshi again comes to the rescue. "I think what Mia is trying to say is that the Snow Carnival brings in the appearance of snow, even when there's no snow," he says, raising his eyebrows at me in a supportive way. I nod gratefully. "And I know you all have so much on your plates right now and that I've never been to a Flurry Winter Festival before," Yoshi goes on, smiling a little. "But we feel strongly about this. People will obviously know there's no snow. We can't pretend that it's there. But we can create the *memory* of snow to replace the snow that is supposed to be there."

"Say more about that, Yoshi," Principal Diaz says. "Are you suggesting we make snow . . . decorations?"

I can't tell if Principal Diaz thinks that's a good idea or not, but I'm happy when Yoshi nods. "Well, maybe something a bit more sophisticated than decorations," he says. "But it's like the way things look like Christmas when you have the lights up. Or Hanukkah when menorahs are in the windows."

I'm shocked when I see Marcus stand up. Maybe he's going to argue that we shouldn't be doing this at all. But then—

"I agree with Yoshi and Mia," Marcus declares. "We need snow at this festival. If that means making paper snowflakes and hanging them around town, we should do it. Nobody is going to think we're trying to pretend it's actual snow, but at least we can all kind of admit that we miss the snow."

It's not until he sits down that I realize my mouth has been hanging open during Marcus's entire speech. I glance over at Lark and she seems just as shocked.

And then Mom gets up. "I think we should bring this to a vote," she starts. "We've been here a long time and it's still a school night for these kids. But I do want to register my support for these ideas. First, I think we should allow them to work on the Snow Carnival, with Maayan reporting back to Anaya for her final approval."

"That works for me," Anaya chimes in.

"And second," Mom continues, "we should think about how to work in the appearance of snow, even if the weather isn't cooperating."

"Who's going to head up the decoration committee?" Principal Diaz asks.

I bristle a bit at the word *decoration* since that makes it seem frivolous. But that's the least of my problems when Soleil looks to each council member, and they all shake their heads. I know each one of them has already been working on their own responsibilities at the festival, just as we have. But I wish—

"Would we be able to do it?" Marcus asks.

Once again, my jaw drops down. This is the most helpful Marcus has ever been about the festival. What changed?

"I think your committee has plenty on its plate," Soleil says.

"Actually, we only have two more days of school left before winter break," Marcus points out, "and we already planned most of the Snow Carnival back in September. With Mia in charge, we've become a pretty creative committee. You should see what Mia had planned for the Snowman Building event."

I can feel my cheeks flush when everyone glances my way.

Soleil glances around the circle again. The council remains quiet, and I try to read their faces.

"Kids, I'm going to need to ask you to head back outside while we take our vote," Soleil says. "Hopefully, it'll only take a few minutes and then we can adjourn the meeting. Apparently, we all have a lot to do."

*   *   *

I don't know how to feel when the five of us are ushered back into the corridor. The festival is still on, I remind myself, no matter what. But everything else that I care about is up in the air. Well, except for the sleigh ride. That's not happening for sure.

I chew on my bottom lip, glancing out the oversize windows that frame the corridor. The sky remains stubbornly clear. The ground remains stubbornly dry. Why can't it snow?

"I wish your dad could just *tell* people it was going to snow," I say to Yoshi.

He frowns at me. "I thought we talked about how my dad doesn't make the weather happen, he just reports on it."

I shake my head. "I know. I just mean that I'm sure it will snow *eventually*. And it would be so much easier if we weren't so worried about when the snow will come. If your dad just *says* the snow is coming . . ."

"Except, as far as we know, it isn't." Yoshi's tone is a little clipped.

"I know." I take a few more steps to the window. I glance at Lark to see if she can jump in and help, but she's busy talking to Kyle and Marcus. "Forget it. I'm not explaining myself properly."

I can't believe it was just last night that Yoshi and I were stuck at Dad's house during the storm. There's a big part of me that wishes I could go back to that moment. That moment when I wasn't thinking about the festival because I had other things on my mind.

Then the door opens and Soleil comes out into the hallway.

"Guys?" she says to us. "The council has reached a decision on your proposal."

Chapter Ten

I hold my breath, and then Soleil smiles.

"The council voted yes!" she exclaims. "We will have the Snow Carnival, and you guys can also be in charge of creating the non-snow snow."

The five of us cheer, and Lark gives her mom a huge hug.

"Mrs. Gonzales is going to look into the insurance issues for the carnival booths, but I don't think that will be a problem," Soleil adds, squeezing Lark tightly. "And I will need you guys to really step up. Marcus, if you are serious about making a push on the decorations, I'm going to need your ideas by Tuesday, first thing. We'll need time to gather the supplies and put them up."

"I'm good with that," Marcus says.

"Okay, lovely. Mia, you'll continue to keep Maayan updated, and she'll work with Anaya," Soleil says with a nod.

Maayan is coming out into the corridor then, along with the rest of the council, including Mom. Maayan gives me a high five, and Mom smiles and puts her arm around me.

"Well done," Mom whispers, and I feel a flutter of pride.

"You guys should go home," Soleil tells me, Marcus, Kyle, and Yoshi. "You have a long couple of days ahead of you, and that's even before the festival starts!"

"Let's go home, too, Mom," Lark says, and Soleil kisses her forehead.

"I need a few more minutes," she says.

Lark frowns. "Mom, come on," Lark implores. "You've been working late every night."

It's like her words take the wind right out of Soleil's sails.

"You're right," she says, her words muffled by a big yawn. "I'm definitely exhausted."

Mom and I say good-bye to Soleil and Lark, and I wave to Marcus and Kyle. I try to look for Yoshi in the crowd, but I see he's off to the side, talking to Principal Diaz.

"Mom, I just need to say one thing—"

"Mia, we've got to go. We're short-staffed, Thierry is trying to manage everything on his own, and two guests checked in right before I left. It's time to go home." Her voice is firm, no room for negotiation.

She buttons her camel winter coat, lifting the collar around her neck to keep out the chill. Without glancing back at me, she begins to walk to the car, so I hurry after her.

It isn't until I'm inside the car that I send a quick text to Yoshi.

Mia Buchanan: Sorry, I had to run. Mom needed to leave. But YAY! YAY! YAY!

A split second later, as though he was watching his phone as well, Yoshi texts back.

Yoshi Pennington: No problem! I saw your mom leading you away. I assume we're going to start working on this tomorrow?

Mia Buchanan: DEFINITELY!

Yoshi Pennington: Ouch. Stop screaming.

Mia Buchanan: Hahahaha. OK, I need to go because I'm only allowed to sit in the front seat if I'm not on my phone. *eye roll* #momrules

Yoshi Pennington: NP. But, is everything OK with Lark?

Mia Buchanan: I think she's worried about her mom. Why?

Yoshi Pennington: OK. I must have misread the situation.

I want to ask him more, but Mom takes my phone and puts it in her purse, so that means no phone until tomorrow. I want to argue, but it's not worth it. Considering #momrules and all.

Monday passes in a rush. While Lark says she "isn't mad at me," she's definitely giving off a frosty air. This frostiness only seems to worsen when I'm accosted by classmates brimming with ideas about the Snow Carnival and snow decorations. Apparently, word got around and everyone has an idea about fake snow. As Lark and I walk through the halls toward our student council meeting, I take out my notebook and pen so I can start to jot down the suggestions.

By the time Lark gives me her hundred thousandth eye roll, I kind of snap.

"I don't get it," I say. We stop in the middle of the hallway and face each other. "We're *supposed* to be brainstorming. Your mom agreed to it!"

Lark scowls at me, dropping her bag on the ground like this might take a while. "Of course she did. It's you. She loves you. That doesn't mean your ideas are good!"

I reel back from the impact of her words, as if they were physical things she hit me with. "You don't think my ideas are good?" I ask, hearing the hurt in my voice.

Lark closes her eyes. She leans against the locker behind her like maybe she's sore or her muscles hurt.

"Are you okay?" I whisper.

She nods, eyes still closed. She opens them slowly but doesn't look in my direction.

"That's not what I meant. It's not that I think your ideas are bad," she explains, her tone still tight. "It's that my mom is so stressed out right now. She's barely sleeping, worrying about what will happen with the festival. And maybe your ideas will work. And maybe they will be amazing. It's just that sometimes I wonder . . ."

Her voice dies down, and then she shakes her head. "Nothing. It's all fine."

"No, say it," I whisper.

She glances up to the ceiling. I can't even remember the last time Lark seemed this down. Sure, she gets tired out, that's normal. Or she overworks her body. But she hasn't seemed this defeated in a long time. Not since she had her operation, and in the months afterward, when she was so frustrated by her progress, by having to relearn all the things she already knew how to do. But I know this is something else.

She presses her lips together and then her eyes meet mine. "Sometimes I wonder if you really get how hard this is for my family. Mom is killing herself trying to make sure this year doesn't bankrupt the town. And then you come in and you're like, 'What if we did this? What if we did that?' Like it's no big deal. Like someone can just do it in an evening and then we'll all go back to school the next morning and magic elves will do all the work. But a lot of the work falls to my mom, and then it just creates stress for me at home, and . . ."

I take in all the words, all the feeling, and instead of arguing, I just nod. Because I get it. I do.

"I know your family is stressed, too, with the inn," Lark says, meeting my gaze. I realize then that I haven't even told her yet that we might be selling it. But now doesn't seem like the best time.

I lean forward to take Lark's hand. Her fingers are tiny, delicate. For someone who is so strong, her body is smaller than most, and I sometimes forget that. I forget that she needs her mom to be a mom and not just the mayor of the town.

"I'm sorry," I say, and squeeze her hand.

"It's fine," she says, but I don't feel like the tension is gone. It's like we've talked about the stuff on the surface, but something is still there. I want to push her on it, but Yoshi walks up to join us.

"Ready for Marcus's decorations meeting?" he asks, and then pauses as he glances back and forth between the two of us. But if anything, Lark looks less happy than before.

She nods and then shrugs with one shoulder. "Let's go."

And she starts walking ahead. Without me.

It turns out that Marcus isn't bad when he's in charge. He's even done some research on snow-based crafts online. He passes around printouts from Pinterest. Some are too expensive or complicated to do, but they certainly help generate more ideas.

"Maybe we could set up those cotton battings that can go on the grass to look like pretend snow," Kyle suggests.

"That's bad for the environment," Maayan chimes in. But I can tell by the way she stares off into space that she's thinking.

"Well, we could get all the stores in town to decorate their windows with snow paintings," Yoshi suggests.

We all nod. Solid idea. But . . .

"There's got to be something more. Something special," I mutter. My eyes scan the library as though something here could jog my thinking. I love the way that Maayan decorates the library little by little every day. Today, the windows have fairy lights bordering them.

"White lights," I say slowly, the idea slowly taking shape. "What if we get a ton of white Christmas lights and . . ."

I saw something like this online. Where was it?

I pull out my phone. Christmas lights wrapped around trees. It takes me a couple of pages before I find the picture

I was searching for. "This," I say, turning the phone toward the group. "It's a zoo in Chicago. Every year, they wrap bare trees in Christmas lights. And while they have a variety of beautiful colors, we could do it with just white lights. It would almost look like . . ."

"Giant snowflakes," Yoshi fills in. "It would be beautiful."

Marcus's and Kyle's and Lark's eyes are as big as Yoshi's and mine. Even Maayan looks excited. I'm not crazy. This could actually work . . .

"How would we get all the Christmas lights? It would cost a ton of money," Kyle asks, and I wrinkle my nose. It's a good question.

"What if we asked stores or families in town to sponsor one tree around the festival area," Lark suggests, and she's smiling. She's really smiling. And if Lark is smiling, it means it could actually happen. "We could even let people put little plaques on the trees with the sponsorship information. They could do it with their own Christmas lights, as long as they're white, or they can buy new ones."

I blink rapidly. I'm not going to cry. This could totally happen, and I'm not going to cry.

"I love this idea," Yoshi says, grinning. "But can I suggest another one to add to it?"

Marcus nods.

"You made me think of it when you mentioned Chicago," Yoshi tells me. "There's this thing where different cities have an animal or something that represents their city."

"Oh yeah, I've heard of that!" Kyle exclaims.

Yoshi nods excitedly. "And they do these special events where they create giant versions of those animals, like almost life-size, and artists decorate the statues and sell them as fund-raisers. I think New York had the cow parade, Toronto had a moose parade, and I remember reading that Jerusalem had giant lions. What if we could do something like that, but with snowflakes?"

"But how would we make giant snowflakes?" Kyle asks, and as much as I want to be cheering on this idea, I have the same question.

"You said that there are tons of artists who come for the festival, right?" Yoshi asks. "What if we gave them the challenge to create snowflakes, and they can be auctioned off at the end of the festival . . ."

"Oh . . ." I breathe. My heart feels like it's too big for my chest. I can just imagine all these different depictions of snowflakes based on the different mediums the artists work in. Like felt snowflakes and glass snowflakes and . . .

"And kids could make cutout paper or plastic snowflakes," Kyle adds, and I'm willing to bet all my money that he feels the same way as I do after seeing the smile that Lark has in store for him.

"I love this idea," Maayan says, already tapping out a message on her phone. "But I think it's unlikely we can get the artists to take part. Artists need much more time to create something like that. But . . . I grew up in Ottawa,

Canada, and there the Winterlude festival is a huge thing," she says, her cheeks flushed. "Ice sculpture contests and skating on the canal . . ."

It sounds amazing. She even pulls up some pictures on her phone to show us. But we all laugh at how bundled up everyone is. "How cold is it there?" Yoshi asks, his brow furrowed like he's scared to hear the answer.

"Really, really cold." Maayan laughs. "But Winterlude is super fun, and it's also where people from all over the world discover BeaverTails!"

The look on all our faces is identical: horror.

"You eat . . . beaver tails?" Kyle whispers.

Kyle is our grade's resident foodie, but even his face is starting to turn a bit green.

Maayan grins. "They're delicious. Especially on a cold day; they're nice and hot. You can put cinnamon and sugar on them, maybe a bit of lemon. Other people put chocolate spread or . . ."

"Stop!" Lark says, one hand pressed against her stomach,

the other holding on to the table. "I think I'm going to be sick."

Maayan tips her head to one side and gives Lark a blank look. "Why . . ." And then her face switches into a wide grin. "Ohhh! I probably forgot to tell you that BeaverTails are named for their *shape,* not for what they're made of. They're just fried dough, pulled into a long oval like a beaver's tail. Totally vegetarian. Vegan, actually, to be precise."

Our shock is quickly replaced by relieved laughter, though I think my face is still a little pale.

"What if we did something like that here?" Maayan continues, giving me a wink. "We already have the food stalls for roasted chestnuts, hot cocoa, soups, and breads. Maybe we can ask one of the bakers to make a fried-dough treat. Though, obviously, we couldn't call it a BeaverTail!"

Lark shakes her head, her braid swishing from one shoulder to another. "We definitely shouldn't."

"What if we made funnel cakes in the shape of snow-flakes?" Kyle suggests. "We can even sprinkle powdered sugar on top to make it look white."

"Yes!" My jump and yell might have been a little intense for our small study room, based on the way it seemed to shock everyone. I flop back on the chair. Maybe I should try to be a tad less dramatic. Whatever.

"I'm glad you like the idea," Maayan says, laughing at my enthusiasm.

"Every year, Bari from Bari's Bakery makes donuts," Kyle says. "I can talk to her about adding this to the menu. She might even let me help her . . ."

Whenever Kyle has come to the inn for group study sessions in the past, he always spends way more time talking with Thierry in the kitchen than studying. Though he claims that he's just doing a different kind of learning.

"Great. I'll discuss the other ideas with Anaya," Maayan says as we wrap up for the day and put on our coats and hats to leave. The six of us walk out of the building together. "I think the Flurry Trees are really doable, and I'm happy to be the organizing force for it," Maayan adds, and I can't help it, I let out a giant sigh. I love the idea of Flurry Trees.

"I'll speak to my mom about all of it, too," Lark says as we all step outside into the cold evening. A tiny beep goes off from her phone. "Oh, and that's her," Lark says, looking up from the text she got. She waves to Soleil's waiting Prius. "Anyone need a ride?"

I almost want to go with her, just so we can continue our conversation, but I also feel like maybe my BFF wants some distance from me.

"A ride would be great," Kyle tells her, a little shyly, which I think is super cute, but I don't let on that I'm thinking this. Besides, Kyle lives pretty near Lark, so it makes sense that he'd go with her.

"I'll come along, too," Marcus offers, and I think I see Kyle's face sag.

Lark, Kyle, and Marcus head for Soleil's car, and Maayan waves good-bye and walks over to the bus stop.

Which just leaves me and Yoshi.

"In the mood for a walk?" he says, and my whole body warms instantly. How does he do that to me?

"I'd love to. I don't think I can sit in a car after all that excitement. I need to be out walking off some of that energy."

"Sounds great," Yoshi says, flipping his collar up. "Let's go."

Chapter Eleven

For the first few minutes, Yoshi and I walk in silence, as though we need a certain distance from school to find our connection.

"So, I have a confession to make," Yoshi finally says. "I totally get why everyone thought BeaverTails sounded gross, and I agree. But here's the thing. I kind of feel the same way about roasted chestnuts."

I stop in my tracks.

"You don't like"—I pause for dramatic effect—"roasted chestnuts? How is that even *possible*?"

He shrugs. "I picture them tasting like mushrooms! All brown and musty and earthy."

I grimace. "I don't even know what you're talking about. Chestnuts are nothing like that. And neither are mushrooms, for that matter!" Thierry would be aghast. "Have you even *had* chestnuts?" I challenge him as I start walking again.

He shrugs. "On Thanksgiving. They're tasteless in stuffing."

I shake my head. "Roasted chestnuts are not like the chestnuts in stuffing. In stuffing they're like a condiment, just put in for an extra taste or texture. Yummy roasted chestnuts in a paper bag are unlike anything else." My stomach growls just thinking about the snack. "Trust me. I can't believe you've never tried them!"

Yoshi glances down at the pavement, and I feel a pang of shame. "I guess they're not that popular in California," I quickly amend. "I mean, I know it's not regular food. It's not like you've never had bread or cheese or milk . . ."

Yoshi laughs. "True. I have had those things. Just not roasted chestnuts."

"So you don't even know if you like them or not," I point out. Hmm. I've never thought of the possibility that someone has never tasted what is the essential taste of my childhood. Could there be other tastes that I take for granted?

"Have you had roasted marshmallows?" I ask.

"Yes!" His eyebrows furrow.

"Do you like them?"

"Of course."

"Okay." I think. "Maple syrup?"

"Yes." He has this odd expression on his face. Like he's trying hard not to be amused by my antics but maybe . . . Maybe he is amused?

"Real maple syrup," I continue, staring into his eyes. "Not the brown corn syrup they serve at pancake houses." I'm really starting to sound like Thierry.

He stares right back at me. "Yes," he says definitively.

"Okay," I accept. "*But* I'm guessing you've never had fresh hot maple syrup that's just been made, poured on top of a plate full of snow until it becomes sticky, and then rolled on a stick?"

His jaw drops. "Tell me you're making that up."

I grin. "Nope. It's delicious. But it's not something you can buy at a store. You have to make it yourself. Experience it in person."

"Really?" Yoshi's looking at me like I'm a crazy person. "I'm guessing this is a Flurry delicacy?"

I nod. "Just wait until March. All the stores in town get the best maple syrup then. You'll see."

Yoshi is no longer staring at me like a crazy person, but his eyes have not left mine. His gaze is thoughtful, and it sends shivers up my spine. Like maybe it means something.

But it can't. It can't possibly mean . . .

I clear my throat. "Okay, so now we know we need to go to the Sugar Shack in March. Or it could be late February, depending on when the sap comes down. Which depends on the weather. Like, when it gets warm. It's this very complicated thing that can totally change based on the year and the fact that it hasn't snowed yet . . ." I'm babbling and I don't even know what I'm saying. All I know is that something is happening here. Something kind of unexpected that makes me want to curl up into a ball but also jump up and squee. At the same time. It's confusing, so words spill out of me instead, like I can build them into a protective shield.

"I'm in," he finally says, interrupting what is apparently an overview of every time I've been to the Sugar Shack, including the time I ate three servings of the syrup sticks and threw up in the car.

Oh my god. I just told Yoshi about the time I threw up in the car and it smelled like syrup.

"Please forget everything I just said," I beg, and this time it's me that is looking away. This is so mortifying.

"I honestly couldn't catch all of it," he says, and there's a bit of a chuckle in his voice. "Though I will be careful not to eat too many syrup sticks."

Oh, good. He caught the important part.

I place my mittens over my face and breathe in the familiar scent of the wool.

I wish I was a little kid and still believed that if I couldn't see someone, they couldn't see me. I'm quite sure Yoshi sees me perfectly right now, but I wish I were invisible.

"Don't be embarrassed," he says. "It was cute."

Cute. He called me cute. Or maybe how I was behaving was cute. I don't even know anymore. How come in real life, you can't take a time-out to pause the action and figure out what's happening? How did we even get here?

Right, chestnuts.

I slowly let the mittens drag down my face and I open my eyes. I was apparently pressing a little too hard on my eyelids because the first thing I see are dancing, colorful spots.

"So, back to roasted chestnuts," I say.

"Right," Yoshi says, smiling. We start walking again, crossing the street and passing Bari's Bakery.

"At the festival," I explain, "there'll be these stands where people will roast the chestnuts on grills. You'll be able to smell them from far away, and it's really the most amazing smell. Like warm fires and wood and winter, all rolled into one."

"That does sound good," Yoshi admits.

I nod. "Yep. The person running the stand scores an X into the chestnut peel before they're grilled," I go on, thinking about what my dad taught me as a kid. "Once the edges of the X have curled back nicely and the chestnut appears brown inside, they grab a scoop of them and fill a small paper bag for you. And then you walk through the festival, eating them. One hand holds the warm bag and it makes your hand sweaty inside your mitten. And you break open the shells with your other hand. And that hand is cold because you can't open the shells with mittens on, except for your fingertips that are burning because the nuts are still hot."

"Why don't you just wait until they cool down before eating them?" Yoshi wonders out loud.

I shrug. "You just don't. They don't taste as good when they cool, though they're still delicious," I hasten to add. "But when they're still a little too hot? They're the best."

"I can see why you love them," Yoshi says. "You might have convinced me. Maybe I'll try them at the festival."

"You'll definitely try them then," I promise as we stop at a crosswalk and wait for the light to change. "But I can also make them for you in the fireplace. They aren't as perfect, but it's also kind of nice not having to freeze and burn your hands at the same time."

"I'd like that," Yoshi says, and the warmth of his words expand my chest.

"If you want . . ." I start and then chicken out. What if he says no? What if he's just being polite? I wish I could talk to Lark about this! "Never mind."

"What?" he asks, and he takes a step closer to me.

"It's silly."

"Tell me," he says, placing his hand on my arm.

My heart races. I drop my arm down, dislodging his hand. Awkward.

"I was going to say that if you wanted, I could make some roasted chestnuts for us before the festival," I say quickly. "Or not. You'll probably be really busy. I could even invite a bunch of people over and we could—"

"That would be great," Yoshi says. "One night this week? When are you free?"

Is this a date? It feels like a date. He's asking me if I'm free one night. But maybe he's just trying to find a time to meet and it isn't a date-date.

Agh!

The light changes to green and we cross the street. "I think tomorrow night might work," I finally manage to say. "We could even meet at my dad's house, since you're right next door and all. Plus, Mom and Thierry get a little crazy at the inn before the festival, so going to Dad's house makes more sense for me. I just need to check with Dad if they have plans, but he's usually up for making a fire. It fits with the Mountain Man vibe he likes to have going."

"Sounds great." Yoshi's smile is open and warm, not at all guarded. I feel my mouth curve into a smile as well, and wonder if it looks the same to him.

"Do you have any thoughts as to who I should invite?" I ask. "Lark? Kyle? Marcus?"

He shrugs. "Up to you. But don't feel like you have to invite them. I mean, unless you want to make it a planning meeting for our festival projects."

"Ugh, no. I think we need a break from that." Just having Lark and Kyle over would be fine, but then it would really feel like this was a double date. Except at my dad's house? And maybe Lark is still mad at me?

This is too confusing.

"The truth is," I fudge, "I may have better luck getting my dad to say yes if there aren't too many people. Because of the littles. They get too worked up and excited when a lot of guests come over."

Yoshi chuckles. "I can see that." He pauses a beat and then adds, "So if your dad is cool with it, we're on for tomorrow night?"

"Yup." I swallow hard. Even though it's so cold I can't feel my face, I'm sweating under my jacket, wool sweater, and long-sleeve shirt.

We've reached the inn, so I wave to Yoshi and hurry toward the door. I hope I can survive until tomorrow.

I text Dad as soon as I get upstairs to my room. As I predicted, he loves the idea of Yoshi coming over so he can teach him how to make a fire and I can introduce him to roasted chestnuts.

I text Yoshi that tomorrow night is a go, and he texts back a thumbs-up emoji.

I grin, sinking down into my bed with my phone in my clammy hands. I know things are still awkward with Lark, but even she has to understand that this is monumental, that I can't be expected to process this on my own.

I send her a text.

> **Mia Buchanan:** So . . . I think something is happening between me and Yoshi.

No reply.

Normally, a text like that would have provoked a series of exclamation marks and shocked emoji faces from Lark, plus possibly a phone call or even a last-minute visit.

But nothing. Maybe she's doing homework. Not that we have much homework, since tomorrow is the last day of school before winter break.

I elaborate.

> **Mia Buchanan:** I mean, I think. I'm not sure. But we were walking home today and talking about the BeaverTails,

which led to a conversation about roasted chestnuts, which led to him saying he'd never had any and me inviting him to Dad's house to make some. And I didn't mean it like a date. But I think he answered it like it was a date. I think. I'm not sure.

I can't believe I just typed all that in a text message. I wish I knew whether Lark was even checking her texts. What if she forgot her phone somewhere and now someone else was reading these messages?

Mia Buchanan: LMK when you get this. I NEED to talk.

But there's no return message.

Chapter Twelve

The next day, I don't manage to get ahold of Lark until lunchtime. I remember that she had a doctor's appointment scheduled for this morning and will be coming in late, so she's not in any of our morning classes.

It's the last day of school before winter break, and everything's a whirlwind. Luckily, our teachers know better than to make us get anything done when all anyone can think about is the festival. Even though I'm splitting my time worrying about the festival, worrying about Lark, and worrying about hanging out with Yoshi tonight at Dad's.

I'm like a ball of worry.

At lunch, I finally see Lark. She, Yoshi, Kyle, Marcus, and I share a table in the cafeteria to finalize the plans for the carnival booths. We need to give them to Maayan before the end of the day so she can pass them along to Anaya to approve.

I try fifteen different times to get Lark alone, but it never happens. She has to leave lunch early to meet with a teacher about a project, and then when I see her in the hall later, I call out to her, but she doesn't seem to hear me. Did she even get my texts last night? I know that sometimes Lark gets so busy with swim practice and climbing that she forgets about her phone, but still.

At the end of the day, we gather in the library for our last student council meeting of the year.

"Good news!" Maayan tells us jubilantly. "The council has approved all the carnival booths!"

It's incredible.

We all cheer and clap, and even Lark and I exchange a high five. Whew.

"Ms. Mackenzie in the woodshop says she can have the

booths ready by midday tomorrow," Marcus reports. "And I talked to Mr. DeShawn in the art room about paint. Basically, if we can get people together tomorrow to paint, everything should be done in one day and dry in time for Friday."

I glance around our little committee. We've really helped the festival stay afloat, and we're getting to do our Snow Carnival. On top of that, Marcus, who was such a pain last week, has turned into one of our hardest workers.

"This is all pretty amazing, you guys," I say. "I can't believe that all this is really happening." I want to make a speech, or say something meaningful, but instead I feel choked up.

"So let's meet up tomorrow, here at the school, for a painting party?" Kyle suggests. "I'll e-mail the rest of the middle school." He already has his phone out, fingers flying.

Maayan nods. "You can gather in the cafeteria tomorrow. I'll discuss it with the janitors, but it should be fine."

Yoshi grins. "This will be fun. I'll come early to set up snacks and a playlist," he offers. "It'll be like a dry run of the carnival."

"That's perfect," Maayan says, and continues on with her update. Apparently, the town council is having a snowflake-making party for little kids on Thursday. Bari's Bakery is even going to be handing out a free donut hole for every snowflake a child makes.

"A free donut hole?" Kyle laughs. "I'm totally in. I can probably make twenty snowflakes."

"Um, it's just for kids," Marcus says.

"I'm a kid," Kyle protests.

"Maybe you can help Bari make them," Lark says, patting his arm.

Huh. I wonder if Lark also has something to update me on . . .

Soon, the meeting is over and everyone is getting up and packing their bags. I try to get Lark's attention unsuccessfully, but she leaves with the others, and I have to stay behind to touch base with Maayan. By the time I get to our lockers, the hallway is empty.

Neither Yoshi nor I have mentioned tonight's chestnut roasting evening. Did I dream it? Are we still on?

But then I get a text message.

Yoshi Pennington: See you at 7!

At Dad's house that evening, I change my clothes three times.

I wish there was clothing that says: *I think I really like you, but I'm scared that you don't think of me that way, and so maybe it's better to just pretend I don't like you so that I'm not embarrassed when the truth comes out?*

I should create a website or an app. Outfits for emotions rather than events. In the magazines Mom keeps on the coffee table at the inn, there are pictures of outfits that supposedly work "From the Desk to the Dance Floor." My outfits would be more like: "From Pretending You Don't Care to Dressing to Impress With One Simple Sweater."

I end up wearing my favorite worn jeans and a comfy gray henley. Apparently, I'm going for the supercasual look, which I accessorize with a pair of pure wool, oversize socks.

This is me pretending I don't need to dress up, I tell myself as I pull my hair into a ponytail.

I'm so lost in thought that I apparently miss Yoshi's knock on the front door. I hear Shannon opening the door and greeting him.

I run out of my room and see Yoshi standing on Dad's doorstep like he did that night of the rainstorm. Only now he's not dripping wet and freezing. He's just wearing his blue jacket and red scarf, his hands in his pockets, looking a little bit nervous, but a lot cute.

"Thanks for having me over," Yoshi tells Shannon, stepping inside. He sees me hovering behind Shannon and waves.

I wave back. Shannon glances at me over her shoulder, giving me a knowing look.

I'm glad she'll be busy putting the littles to bed soon. Otherwise she might hang around and say something potentially embarrassing.

Then again, there's Dad I have to worry about, too.

Thankfully, Dad is just focused on the fireplace at first. He takes Yoshi through the steps of building a fire while I record (with their permission) a time-lapse video of the whole thing on my phone. The benefit of shooting the video? It gives me something to do instead of just being nervous.

But finally, the fire is roaring and it's warm enough for me to shrug off the afghan I was hiding underneath. I breathe in deeply, the smell of burning wood like a balm to my anxiety. Yoshi takes a seat beside me on the couch.

Dad glances back and forth between us. "So, I'm going to go to my workshop." He scans the room as though looking for possible ways to hide in plain sight and keep watch over us. I can tell he's one second away from just sitting in between us on the couch. My stomach twists. I almost wish Shannon were here instead because she'd probably be more subtle about it all. But she's busy bathing the littles and getting them ready for bed.

"Well, I guess we'll get started on making the chestnuts," I tell Dad at last.

"Yep," Yoshi says.

"We'll be fine," I add, trying to give Dad the hint.

Dad nods and rakes his fingers through his hair. "Okay, I'll be back. In a bit. So make sure . . ." He pauses and appears to be searching for words. "Make sure the fire is okay."

"Okay, Dad," I say. It's actually a little bit funny that he seems nervous. It's almost enough to make me forget my own nervousness.

Dad heads out of the room, and I hear him mutter to himself, "I can't believe I'm going to go through this with four kids."

Yoshi and I both stare straight forward until Dad is gone. And then, almost as if we'd planned it, we both burst out laughing.

"Oh my god, that was painful," I choke out through laughter.

"I almost *left* just to put him out of his misery," Yoshi admits.

I glance over at him and smile. "I'm glad you didn't," I say.

"Me too," he says.

And then the silence gets super awkward superfast.

"So, I can show you how to make the chestnuts—" I say, just as he says: "Can I see the video you made?"

And then we chuckle. Okay, we can do this.

"How about video first and then chestnuts?" I ask.

"Sounds good."

Miraculously, I manage to show Yoshi how to score the chestnuts and roast them in the pan over the fire without injuring either of us. Dad comes to check on us twice (okay, three times), and he says he approves of my chestnut-roasting skills.

Instead of eating the chestnuts as they come out of the pan, like I usually do despite the fact that they wind up burning my tongue, I wait until they've cooled down enough to handle. Then I show Yoshi how to peel the shells back. The smell is so delicious.

Once we've both cracked open our first chestnut, but before we've tasted them, I give him an intense look.

"Just so you know," I say, "I'm not sure we can be friends if you don't like roasted chestnuts."

I don't smile and neither does he. "I totally understand," he says, and then we both pop the chestnuts into our mouths at the same time.

I close my eyes to enjoy my first fire-roasted chestnut of the winter. When I open my eyes again, it's clear that there won't be any problems. Because Yoshi is already on his second one.

We accidentally-on-purpose eat almost all the chestnuts as we sit by the fire and laugh. Yoshi tells me a hilarious story about the time he and his best friend from California, Paz, decided to enter a hot dog–eating competition at a local fair. They ate five hot dogs each and then promptly threw them up. I'm laughing so hard at Yoshi's description of getting all competitive with these professional hot dog eaters that I wind up a little too close to the fire for anyone's comfort. And I lose a chestnut.

"This is getting dangerous!" I jokingly admonish him after I move away from the fire.

"I don't want your dad to think we need to be supervised," Yoshi agrees. I press my lips together to try to prevent them from stretching into the biggest Cheshire Cat grin on the planet.

I can finally admit to myself that I have a huge *c-r-u-s-h* on Yoshi Pennington. And for the first time, I wonder if he really might feel the same way about me.

Chapter Thirteen

Usually I wouldn't want to be at school on the first day of winter break. But on Wednesday, I can't wait to go back for the booth-painting party. First, though, I help Mom string up the white Christmas lights on the trees outside the inn (so we can have our own pretend snowflakes). But as soon as we're done with that and with lunch, I dash over to school.

The cafeteria looks incredible. Yoshi, as promised, arrived early and transformed it into its own version of a winter wonderland. There are the white Christmas lights strung up everywhere, a bunch of paper snowflakes taped to the walls, and an entire playlist blasting songs about snow. Yoshi really went above and beyond with the setup.

Most of the middle school is here, and Kyle really got the word out. There are kids with snowflakes painted on their cheeks, others wearing ugly and not-as-ugly Christmas sweaters, and a good number of kids with spray-painted white hair and white nails. Claudia, a girl in our grade who can usually be found on the basketball court, is even wearing a Snow White costume. It's hilarious.

I spot Yoshi at the back of the room, talking to a group of sixth-grade girls who very definitely have their own c-r-u-s-h on him. Which I totally get since he looks super cute. His dark hair is covered by a blue bandana, which would look totally hip if he wasn't also wearing a snowflake tiara on top of it.

Yep. Yoshiki Pennington is wearing a sparkly snowflake crown. And because it's clearly meant for a head much smaller than his, every time he moves, he tips over the crown. It's kind of adorable. He's also sporting some paper cutout snowflakes, all pinned on his dark jeans and blue T-shirt ensemble. I couldn't look that cool if I tried. Exhibit A: the white fuzzy sweater I'm wearing that is causing me to rapidly overheat.

I scan the rest of the room. Everything is organized in each corner, courtesy of Marcus. Each wooden booth is already assembled, accompanied by a drawing of what the front should look like. It's basically one giant paint-by-numbers exercise since Marcus has even penciled in the picture on the wood.

There are two beanbag toss/snowball toss booths: One is shaped like a snowman with big holes for little kids, and the other has a picture of a snowball fight painted on it, with holes in the board where the snowballs can fit . . . if you have great aim. I might stick to the little kid game.

There's also a snowball bowling game, a snowball bulls'-eye target game, snowball golf, a tic-tac-toe snowboard, a frozen bubble blowing booth, and a graffiti station where kids can use nontoxic paint in squeeze bottles to make designs on the snow. And, of course, a snow obstacle course.

"This is amazing," I gush when Yoshi meets me in the middle of the room. It's only then that I even notice he has a snack table set up with snowflake cookies and brownies topped with white chocolate chips. "When did you make all this happen?"

"I came early this morning. I wanted it to be a surprise."

He is so thoughtful, I'm basically speechless.

"So, are you here to paint or did you just want to see what was happening?" Yoshi asks, and I almost miss his words because "There's No Day Like a Snow Day" by Runaway Cat Train comes up on his playlist and everyone starts cheering and doing the silly snow dance.

"Can Mia and I paint the snowball toss backgrounds?" Marcus asks, coming up from behind me.

"Of course! Go for it." And then Yoshi's dancing toward the middle of the room again, like he's not remotely jealous.

"*No day like a snow day,*" Yoshi sings along with the music. "*No day like a day with you.*"

I allow myself a tiny glance up at his face, and he's looking at Claudia, who is apparently singing the duet with him.

No big deal. Totally no big deal.

Marcus and I take a seat at a table and paint quietly.

"Why did you want to paint with me?" I finally ask.

Marcus looks at me like I have three heads. "Why not?"

"Because you don't like me." I can't believe the words coming out of my mouth. But between Lark still being weird—I haven't even seen her here yet—and Yoshi singing with Claudia, I'm a mess. "I'm sorry, I didn't mean to say that."

Marcus puts down the paintbrush. "I do like you."

"Then why do you always seem like you're mad at me?" I don't know where I got this confidence from. Two weeks ago, I would never have said any of these words to Marcus.

"I'm sorry," Marcus says quietly. I lean forward because I almost can't hear him over the music. "It's just been tough since I moved back to Flurry. But it's not about you." He stares at me intently, his dark eyes not blinking. "Do you believe me?" he asks.

"I guess," I say. "But why are things tough?"

Marcus dips his brush in the green paint. "When we moved to Springfield, I hated it and I just wanted to move back to Flurry. I missed my friends. I missed my house. I even missed school."

I laugh because the Marcus I knew before he left was never a big fan of school.

He smiles wryly. "It's true. But then, a few years ago, when Dad said we were moving back, I didn't *want* to come back. I had friends in Springfield by then. And even though I used to live here, everything feels different now."

He shakes his head and dips his paintbrush in the water. I don't tell him that he hadn't actually painted the green. It doesn't seem important.

"Have you tried talking to Yoshi?" I ask. "He's new to the town. Newer than you, even." I smile. I don't want to tell Marcus everything that Yoshi told me, but I think maybe the two of them could help each other.

Marcus shrugs.

"You should try. He's a good guy and he's also dealing with moving here, although your situations are different."

"Thanks," Marcus says. "I'm sorry if I've been hard to deal with."

"It's okay," I tell him. "For what it's worth, it's good to have you back in Flurry. I did miss our epic snowball fights."

"Only because you always won!" Marcus says, making a fake angry face.

Marcus and I spend the next hour laughing at childhood memories and painting the snowball toss stands. It turns out that Marcus really hasn't changed that much from the boy I'd known so many years ago. He'd just seemed different. Apparently, he can even still burp many of the letters of the alphabet.

When we're not reminiscing, I try to focus on the painting. I'm glad that Marcus created a picture on the plywood, because I can barely paint the white snowdrifts without messing them up.

"Maybe you should only work on the snowman painting since it's mostly just a big white surface," Marcus suggests, and I wish I had a snowball in my hands. I would make sure I didn't miss. Instead, I just stick out my tongue.

"I do the organizing around here. I can't be expected to be good at everything," I retort instead.

"Apparently not," Marcus teases.

"How's it coming?" Yoshi asks a while later, sauntering over to check on our work.

"Pretty well," I say, lifting my arms and stretching. I happen to glance up and see Lark and Kyle on the other side of the gym. I can't believe I didn't see them come in. Or did they not see me?

"Lark and Kyle have been here this whole time?" I say in surprise.

"Yup," Yoshi says. "They actually helped me create a giant cardboard snowman so we can use our whole photo booth setup with a pretend snowman. Maayan totally okayed it, just in case you're worried. If people can't build their own snowmen, at least they can still take silly pictures with a pretend one."

"Nice," Marcus says.

I nod, my eyes fixed on Lark and Kyle. It's not possible that Lark doesn't see me. Is she really ignoring me? Hoping I wouldn't notice her?

"Be right back," Marcus says, getting up and flashing us his paint-stained palms. "Need to wash my hands."

He takes off, leaving me alone with Yoshi. Normally, that would make me happy, but I'm too distracted by Lark.

"So I have an update," Yoshi says. "I didn't want to tell you until I was sure I could get them, but I thought we could create a little village at the carnival. I've talked with a bunch of families about donating those big outdoor plastic houses. We could put them all in one area, and maybe create a border around them with tables or benches or something so that the kids can play inside them." His eyes meet mine. "I know it's not on the original list of the carnival activities, but I saw it online and it seemed really cute—"

"I think it's a neat idea," I interrupt. "But what's the connection to snow?"

He shrugs. "I was thinking since it might wind up snowing, it'll look like a mini version of a ski village. And if it doesn't snow, we can stick some Christmas lights and big snowflakes on the houses."

"It sounds cute." I can see the appeal of the area, and if parents can watch their own kids while they play in an enclosed space, it could be great.

"But wait." I am running through Yoshi's words, and I can't believe I was so freaked out about Lark ignoring me that I didn't hear what he'd said. "What do you mean it might wind up snowing?"

Yoshi bites his bottom lip, worrying it between his teeth. "I thought you knew. Earlier it looked like we could get snow on the Monday after the festival. But now it looks like the snow that was supposed to hit farther south is actually going to come up here. Something about wind patterns and cold air and warm air. I tried to get my dad to explain it to me, but I couldn't really understand—"

"Wait. *What?* It might snow on the festival?" I cry.

What does it mean if we get snow? Does it change the plan? We're now doing all this work to make the *fake* snow for the Snow Carnival . . .

"It's looking more likely. But they don't know for sure," Yoshi replies. "Predicting snow is one of the hardest aspects of weather forecasting. It seems easy, right? Water falling from the clouds. But if water freezes on its way down at a certain level, it will make giant snowflakes, which will result in . . ."

I know Yoshi's still talking, but I can't hear his words anymore. It could snow after all. Is this good or is this bad?

"I need to tell Lark," I interrupt, getting to my feet. "She needs to tell her mom. We need to figure out—"

"Lark knows," Yoshi says. "That's why I thought you knew."

"I didn't," I snap. Why didn't Lark tell me? Why didn't she text me about it right away? Did she think I knew already?

"When did you find out?" I demand, and Yoshi shrinks back.

"Last night, when I got home from your dad's house," he says quietly.

"So Lark knows and Soleil knows, and that means tons of people probably know. But at the same time, you don't actually know whether it will or won't snow."

"It looks like—" Yoshi starts, but I start backing away.

"Your dad is the weatherman. How is it that this is coming as a surprise to us? Shouldn't he have known something like this was coming?" I ask.

"It doesn't work like that," Yoshi says, his eyes narrowing. "I told you—"

"I even said the other day that he should just pretend we're getting snow, and you told me that he wouldn't do that!"

"Because he wouldn't. He reports on what he sees, not what we want him to see." Yoshi frowns at me. Yesterday things finally felt like they were going in the right direction, and now everything is upended.

"Whatever." I know that I should calm down, but tears threaten to fill my eyes. "I need to go."

Except, I don't go. I walk over to where Lark and Kyle are arranging the cardboard snowman.

"Hey, guys." I don't even pretend to smile. "Lark, can I talk with you for a minute?"

She follows me to the side of the cafeteria where there are fewer people who might overhear us.

"What's up?" she asks.

"I hear it might *snow*?" My voice is hushed.

"Yup. I figured you knew since you check the weather apps every hour."

I groan. Ever since I stopped being worried that the festival would be canceled, I stopped checking the weather apps. "I didn't know."

"Oh." Lark glances at the ground. "Sorry."

Okay, so at least she wasn't purposefully keeping it from me.

"If it might snow, why are we working on all this fake snow stuff?" I ask, waving my hand around.

I can't tell if Lark's rolling her eyes, because she's still staring at the ground. "I don't think they know if the snow is coming for sure. They can't tell yet if it will be freezing rain or good packing snow or just a thin layer."

I remember Yoshi's comment about the different types of snow and how rain freezing at different points changes things. Why can't computers just tell us this stuff?

I sigh. "Is there any chance you want to get out of here and come hang out at the inn with me?" I ask Lark. "Thierry is making chili . . ."

Lark glances around the cafeteria. "I don't think I should leave right now. I have to finish helping Kyle with the snowman."

"Please? We haven't talked in a while, and I really need your help figuring some stuff out."

Lark's eyes flick to my face and then go back down to the floor. "I want to stay here for a while longer. Can we just talk another time?"

"Another time? Lark, we haven't talked in forever!"

"No, Mia," she snaps. "These days, you talk all the time. Usually either about the festival and how important it is that it happens, or about Yoshi. Well, news flash: The festival is not just about you, and either tell Yoshi how you feel or don't."

I take two steps back, shocked at the words coming out of my best friend's mouth.

"I'm s-sorry," I stammer.

Lark rolls her shoulders forward and puts her hands over her face. "No. I'm sorry. I shouldn't have said it like that." She pauses and drops her hands. "Maybe I just need a little break from all of it, okay?"

I'm trying to process her words, but I don't know what to say. "You mean, like a break from me?" I ask, my throat tightening.

Lark doesn't answer, and that's answer enough.

Finally, I turn around, grab my coat from where I left it on a chair, and walk out of school. I don't run, because I'm half hoping that Lark will stop me, but she doesn't. So I walk out into the cold afternoon, my mind blank.

Chapter Fourteen

I make my way home in a daze. Thank goodness I don't live far, because I don't actually remember crossing streets or walking past the various landmarks between school and the inn.

Lark and I might not be best friends anymore. I've probably ruined everything with Yoshi. It may or may not snow this weekend, and I don't know what that means for the festival. And for some odd reason, Marcus and I are back to being friends.

Everything is upside down.

I reach the back entrance of the inn and start to open the door. But then I spot Mom and Thierry sitting together on stools at the kitchen counter. I pause, watching them from outside for a moment. Mom's wearing a dark red silk blouse paired with black slacks and a pair of low black heels. It doesn't matter that she and Thierry are probably just having a cup of tea alone. Mom's the only person I know who wears yoga pants only at yoga.

Unlike Shannon, who would wear yoga pants to church if she was the churchgoing type. Kind of like me.

Thierry, of course, is wearing his chef's whites, though his toque is on the counter beside him.

Why are they even sitting here like this? Usually, in the days before the festival, they're frantically running around, Mom dealing with guests out front and Thierry planning menus with his staff and whipping up treats. Usually, it's madness. Right now it's . . . strangely calm.

Is that because everyone has canceled and the inn is empty? I swallow hard.

I'm about to step all the way inside when I hear Thierry's voice.

"*Chérie*," he's saying to Mom, "do you ever let yourself think about what it would be like if we didn't have the inn to worry about? We could travel, take Mia to all the places we used to talk about going to. We've never even taken her to Haiti, to see where I grew up. We're always tied to the inn."

Mom leans her head down on Thierry's shoulder, both of their backs to me.

I step all the way into the kitchen now. It might be warm in here, but I feel like I have ice running through my veins.

"No," I say before I have a chance to think about my words.

Mom and Thierry shift on their stools, turning to face me.

"Mia," Mom says. "I didn't hear you come in."

I search both their faces for a sign of what's going on, but I can't tell anything. They both look tired, but . . . that's it. Thierry's large hand is covering Mom's, and it's only when I get closer that I see what's spread out on the counter.

Flyers printed with the words FOR SALE and lots of

photographs. I look closer. They're real estate listings for properties in the Northeast. Six different places for sale.

Six places for sale *not* here in Flurry.

Which means we are selling this inn and moving?

"No," I repeat.

Mom frowns and glances over at Thierry, who also seems puzzled. It's hard to tell, though, because I can't see that well through the tears in my eyes.

Not after everything. Not after I did everything I could to save the festival.

"Honey—" Mom starts, but I back away.

"I can't. No. I just . . ." And this time I run through the kitchen and the front of the inn, past Alice at the desk, and then across the garden to our cottage.

I just can't anymore.

Unlike Lark, Mom does follow me. I barely have enough time to fling myself on my bed before she's rapping on my door.

She doesn't wait for me to answer. She comes in and sits beside me.

"Mia, we need to talk," she says as her fingers rake gently through my hair.

I curl my body forward, wishing she'd just leave me alone. Isn't there a guest who needs to be checked in? Or a crisis that needs dealing with? Or did she already sell the inn, so there's nothing to worry about?

I know realistically that isn't possible, but I can't stop the sobs. I can't deal with everything falling apart like this.

"You saw the real estate listings?" Mom asks after a few minutes.

I push my head farther into my pillow. We can't sell the inn and move. We can't.

"You know they're just for research, right?"

I lift my head and turn my face toward her.

"Research?" I echo.

Mom nods. "I asked our real estate agent to send me some

listings for comparable inns in the region, so that if we need to take out a second mortgage, we can use those comps to help us set a value for the inn."

My heart drops again.

"So, we *are* selling the inn?" I whisper.

"We're not," Mom says.

I hate the fact that she's lying to me, that she's treating me like I'm a baby. I grip the duvet tighter. "I heard you and Thierry just now, talking about how nice it would be if you didn't need to worry about the inn."

"Oh, honey." Mom takes my hand in her two cool ones. "Sometimes grown-ups daydream about what it would be like not to have responsibilities, what it would be like if we were free to go where we please, sit on beaches or travel through Europe. But we aren't thinking about giving up the inn in order to do that."

"But last week," I argue, "I heard you telling Thierry that you'd looked into selling the inn." My voice is a near whisper, like saying the words too loudly will make them real.

Mom smiles and shakes her head. "You should stop eavesdropping, hon, and just ask more questions. I'll always be honest with you." She pauses and adds, "Yes, for a moment there, I had considered the possibility of selling the inn. Money *has* been a little tight this year, and you know me, I always like to plan ahead. That's why I talked to our real estate agent. But it's not something Thierry and I need to do. Or *want* to do."

I nod, taking in her words. I believe her now. She wasn't lying to me before. I exhale a breath, and Mom continues.

"Thierry and I love this inn, and as hard as it is to run it sometimes, we enjoy it so much. We're able to work together, side by side. But more importantly, this is our home. Yours and mine and Thierry's."

I curl up until my head rests on Mom's shoulder. Her arms wrap around me, and I let out the tears that have been accumulating all this time.

"So, you *aren't* selling the inn?" I ask, just to triple-confirm. "Is it because the festival is back on?"

"No, we're not going to sell the inn," Mom says. "Is that why you've been so anxious about the festival, because you thought we'd lose the inn if the festival didn't happen?"

I nod into her shoulder. "I was scared that we'd have to move somewhere and I'd be far away from Dad and Shannon and the littles. I wouldn't be able to travel back and forth as easily, and I wouldn't feel at home in either place . . ." I feel the tears threatening to return. As though she can tell, Mom rubs my back like she used to when I was little.

"And I wanted the festival to happen so I could go on the sleigh ride," I admit.

Mom laughs a full-out belly laugh. "Oh, honey. Listen, if we were seriously thinking about moving, you better believe we'd talk to you about it. More importantly, though, living close to your dad is a priority. He's no longer my husband, but our lives will always be connected through you. And I'm not going to do anything to put a strain on you like that. Not if I can help it. And your dad and Shannon feel the same way. As does Thierry."

The relief I feel is all-consuming, even though we're not out of the woods by any sense. "Did you hear it might snow for the festival after all?"

Mom sighs. "I did. Living in Vermont is always a weather adventure. Do you remember that Grandma used to always say that if you don't like the weather, wait five minutes, and it will change?"

I smile. "No."

"It'll be okay," Mom says. "We'll make it work. And about that sleigh ride?" She pats my hand. "You're still the junior coordinator of the festival, no matter what. And hey, we can stage our own sleigh ride and our own photo another time this winter. You do deserve to have your picture down there in the living room."

I laugh, feeling sheepish but also much, much better. "Thanks, Mom."

She stands up, dusting invisible pieces of lint from her pants. "I should head downstairs. Oh. And I almost forgot.

Lark called earlier and said she was going to stop by. She should be here any minute."

"Wait." I sit up. "Lark said she was coming over?"

"Your best friend, Lark?" Mom says with a frown. "The one you spend all your time with? Yes, she said she was heading over."

"When did she call?" It was probably earlier in the day, before we had our fight.

"Maybe ten minutes before you got home? She said she tried your cell phone, but nobody answered, but she was just going to wait for her dad to pick her up at school and then she'd come over. I might have mentioned that Thierry was making chili."

"But—"

Mom's phone beeps with a text and she glances at the screen. "Ah, Thierry says Lark's here. Do you want her to come to the house, or do you want to meet her in the inn?"

"Ummm . . ." I can't figure out which will be best. I guess Lark wouldn't be coming over if she hated me and didn't want to talk to me ever again. But maybe it would be better if we were near Mom and Thierry because then she wouldn't get mad at me in front of them . . .

Mom's phone beeps with another text. "No worries. She's coming here."

I've never been so nervous to see my best friend before.

Thankfully, I have just enough time to wash my face so I look a little less like I've been crying. I meet Lark downstairs in our tiny sitting room. While Lark can get up and down the stairs, she doesn't love doing it. Especially not when she's been on her feet all day.

"Hey," she says when I get downstairs.

"Hey." I take a seat on the opposite end of the couch from her.

I cannot imagine my life without Lark as my best friend. I feel like I'd be losing a part of myself.

"I tried to go after you when you left school, but you were going too fast," she explains.

"Oh." So she did come after me. "Sorry."

"You don't need to apologize."

There's silence.

"I'm really sorry I said all those things in the cafeteria," Lark starts.

"No, I'm sorry—"

Lark puts her hand up. "Mia, let me talk."

I nod.

"I'm sorry I freaked out on you," Lark continues. "The truth is, I've been frustrated, and I let everything build up, and then I just exploded all over the place."

"Frustrated with me?" My stomach hollows as I wait for her to say no, that it has nothing to do with me. But she doesn't shake her head. She nods.

"You're my best friend in the whole world," she says, and now it's her eyes that are filling with tears. "But I feel like over the past couple of weeks, you've been so focused on the festival and on Yoshi, and I don't know where I fit in all that."

I frown. I want to tell her that she always fits in everywhere. "I know I have been distracted," I say. "But mostly it's because I've been terrified Mom and Thierry were going to sell the inn," I explain. "I thought if I could save the festival, that maybe I could save the inn."

Lark blinks rapidly. "Really? Why didn't you *tell* me?"

"Because somehow I thought if I did, it would make it more real." I shrug. "Plus, it never seemed like the right time."

"You can always tell me anything," Lark insists. She frowns, looking really worried. "So *are* they gonna sell the inn?"

I shake my head. "It turns out that they were thinking about it, but they aren't going to right now."

Lark nods, relief crossing her face. "So we've both been worrying about our moms," she says with a chuckle.

"I'm sorry I didn't tell you," I say.

"It's okay," Lark says. "I'm sorry I was being weird all this time." She bites on her bottom lip.

I feel like she still hasn't told me about the bigger issue, the one that's harder to talk about. "What else has been frustrating you?" I ask.

Lark stretches her neck from side to side. "It's about Yoshi," she says at last.

My stomach flips over. "Yoshi?" I echo. Wait. Does *Lark* like Yoshi? Have I been totally blind to that fact? Oh God. What if she does, and she's been jealous and—

"I don't like him!" Lark clarifies, because she's always sort of been able to read my mind. She gives me a smile and an eye roll, and I relax somewhat. "It's more that . . . I suddenly felt like you were moving on without me. Because of Yoshi."

"B-but—" I splutter, confused. "You were always the one telling me to admit to Yoshi how I felt! Not that I've done that," I amend. "But I thought you, I don't know . . . supported my crush?" I laugh, because it sounds silly.

"I do," Lark insists, her eyes wide. "It's just that, when you and Yoshi actually started spending all this time together, and you started having these intense feelings . . . it made me feel kind of down about myself. Because *I* don't feel like that about anybody."

"I keep telling you that Kyle likes you." I take Lark's hands from her lap and put them between mine.

"I know that Kyle likes me. We've talked about it."

"Wait. You *have*?" I'm about to drop Lark's hands, but then I don't.

"Yes. And it's super awkward because I really like him, but I don't like him like *that*. I don't really know what 'like that' even means."

"But maybe you could—"

"But I don't want to," Lark says, this time more emphatically. "If I told you Marcus liked you, would you turn around and like him back?"

I shake my head.

"It's the same thing. I like Kyle a lot, but I don't want him to like me as more than a friend. Because it makes me feel guilty that I don't feel the same way."

"Oh." I can't believe I didn't think of it like that. Especially since it's exactly what I've been worried would happen between me and Yoshi. "I guess I just thought that it would be so perfect if you liked Kyle and I liked Yoshi and then—"

"And that's the problem." Lark slips her hands from mine, and I reach to get them back, but she shakes her head. "Sorry, but your hands are getting sweaty."

I laugh. It's the first totally normal thing she's said.

"I know it would be easier if we were both going through the same thing at the same time," Lark goes on, "but I can't pretend to have a crush on someone just because I want to be the same as you. Which doesn't mean that you can't like Yoshi. Obviously you can. But I need you to remember when you talk about it that we're not going through the same thing."

"I will remember that," I say. "Thank you for explaining everything." I place my arm around Lark's shoulders and pull her into a hug. "I was scared you didn't want to be friends with me anymore."

"Oh, please. You couldn't lose me if you tried. You're stuck with me."

"Promise?" I say as Mom comes into the sitting room.

"Promise," Lark says, hugging me back tightly.

"Sorry to interrupt, girls," Mom says then. "Anyone in the mood for Thierry's chili?"

There's no question that Lark and I are totally on the same page about Thierry's chili.

Chapter Fifteen

When I wake up the next morning and look out my window, I'm greeted by a sight that is so unbelievable, I have to blink several times. After weeks of hoping to wake up to snow, I didn't really think it would happen.

But it's snowing outside. Big fat flakes, the ones that create light and airy snowdrifts that you sink into, are falling from the sky. It's the picturesque type of snow, the kind where you can see each flake individually, like everything is moving in slow motion.

It's the perfect Vermont snow.

Except . . . What does it mean for the festival?

Mom knocks on my door and sticks her head in the room.

"You're awake. Good." She takes a few steps in, her smile wide. "I guess you've seen the weather."

"Yup." I grab my phone. "I should call Lark. See what Soleil is saying."

Mom leans against my doorframe. "I just heard from Soleil, actually. The town council is asking people to meet at the Market Square by nine o'clock. I need to stay here because we have guests on their way, but I can imagine there'll be a lot to do. Maayan can update you when you get down there."

I glance at the time on my phone. Since it's winter break, I haven't been doing my elaborate alarm setups, so I've been sleeping late. And now it's five minutes to nine!

I don't think I've ever gotten ready so fast. There's gorgeous snow outside, and we have a festival to set up—and only one day to do it.

* * *

It feels like the entire town is assembled in the Market Square. Snow is still falling, coating the ground and everyone's jackets, hats, and scarves.

I push my way through the crowds, and I find Lark up front, near Anaya Sodhi, who is holding a bullhorn.

"Good, you made it," Lark whispers to me. "My mom said she called your mom."

I nod and focus on what Anaya is saying.

"If you're working on the ski races, meet Mr. Han in front of the bakery," she says through the bullhorn. "You will get your instructions there."

"I thought you wanted the people setting up for the craft fair to meet at the bakery," Mrs. Sollinger shouts. I catch Lark's eye and we grin. Trust Mrs. Sollinger to notice these things.

"Those volunteers aren't due to arrive for another hour," Anaya says. "But thank you for your concern."

Lark and I start to giggle. As I watch the crowds get organized, my heart swells with pride. There's something so special about this quirky little town that drives itself crazy trying to create a festival dedicated to snow.

Just then I notice Marcus and Kyle making their way toward us, closely followed by Yoshi. He's wearing an amazingly stylish pair of blue, green, and yellow snow pants, with a matching jacket. He doesn't seem to have spotted us yet because he's focusing so hard on not toppling over. I remember how we left things yesterday at the school gym, and I tense up.

"I can hear your heart beating out of control from over here," Lark whispers, and I put my arm around her shoulders.

Before the boys can reach us, Maayan appears at our side, wearing cute earmuffs and listening intently to Anaya.

"Snowshoe Race folks, you're meeting at the corner of Maple and Foster!" Anaya calls. "If you have your white lights for wrapping trees, bring them to the volunteers. If you want them back, please make sure to put your name on them."

"We're still doing the Flurry Trees?" I ask Maayan, and she winks.

"Oh, we're doing a ton of things."

Marcus, Kyle, and Yoshi finally reach us—Yoshi still looking unsteady on his feet—and Maayan explains everything to us. Basically, the town council decided to keep all the events: old *and* new. So store windows are still being decorated with snowflakes, and trees are still being wrapped in white lights, even though there's already a good several inches of snow on the ground.

Most importantly, the Snow Carnival is still on. But only if we feel we can run both the carnival *and* Snowman Building.

"We get to do both?" I swallow hard.

"Do you think you can handle both?" Maayan asks.

I glance at my committee around me.

"What do you guys say?" I ask them.

"I say we do both," Marcus shouts before anyone else can respond. I grin.

"I'm in," Kyle says.

"Lark?" I ask, and my BFF looks at me like I'm crazy.

"Of course."

"Yoshi?" I glance at him, feeling awkward. I wish we could have a moment alone to talk about what happened yesterday.

"Happy to help," he says, but he doesn't actually seem that happy.

I need to fix this.

"Great," Maayan says. "And there are two pieces of good news. One is that, due to the unexpected weather changes, the council decided that you won't need to open either event until Saturday morning. Tomorrow—Friday—will just be for the ski races and the food trucks and craft fair."

"Whew," I say. We could definitely use the extra time.

"The other good news?" Maayan goes on, waving over a group of kids nearby. "I've got a crew of eighth graders who can help out. With the understanding that you guys are in charge."

We're in charge of eighth graders? This might be the best day ever. If only things felt right with Yoshi . . .

Okay. Time to focus. First, festival.

I decide that we'll split into two groups to handle the two different events, and I'll go back and forth between each one.

"Yoshi and Marcus, can you guys lead the team for the Snow Carnival?" I ask. "Kyle and Lark, can you handle Snowman Building?"

Everyone nods. Yoshi and Marcus head off to their station, joining the eighth-grade volunteers.

"Is that okay with you?" I whisper to Lark while Kyle is busy talking to Maayan.

"Totally fine," she whispers back. "It's good to be partners with someone who knows exactly what I need help with and what I can do on my own. Less explaining for me."

"Sounds good." I grin. "Have fun, and don't be too bossy with the eighth graders."

"It's a good thing I love you," she shouts at me over her shoulder, heading toward Kyle.

"I love you, too!" I yell after her.

I go to check on Marcus and Yoshi, who are still waiting for the paint to dry on the various booths. We work together to create the chalet village, which is totally adorable and will be a huge hit. And then we mark out all the places where the booths need to be placed to make sure there's enough room for the different carnival events. It isn't until it's almost dark that we're able to move the booths into the space. But it looks so amazing. Better than I could have dreamed.

"You did this," I tell Yoshi as we walk over to check on Kyle and Lark and the Snowman Building station. Marcus has stayed behind with the booths to perfect everything.

"We all did," Yoshi says, his voice still quiet.

"No." I shake my head. "You're the one who offered to help from the get-go, who talked me through everything. You made me feel like it wasn't impossible, like you believed that this could work. Tomorrow, when kids start coming to the Snow Carnival, you should remind yourself that you did this. You're an essential part of Flurry."

Yoshi stops walking and turns to face me. "You don't need to say that." His eyes are serious, none of the lightness I'm used to seeing there. I want to tell him that I like him, that I like him more than a friend and it's okay if he doesn't like me like that. That I want him to know that he's amazing.

But first, there are more important things to say. "I'm really sorry I freaked out on you yesterday in the cafeteria. It wasn't right."

Yoshi stares down. "It's okay," he finally says. "Do you mind if we sit for a minute? Or should we first go to Snowman Building and make sure everything is done there?"

"Nah," I say, walking the few steps to a snow-covered bench. "Lark and Kyle can totally handle it."

We both brush off the snow with our gloves and then plop onto the bench. The snowflakes are still falling gently all around us.

"The snow is really pretty," Yoshi admits. "I can see why people are so into it."

I giggle. "It is."

Yoshi falls quiet again. Even though I've only known him for a few months, I know now that this is his way to tell a story. Whereas I burst out with everything at once, a wild torrent, Yoshi pauses before he says something important. Like he first wants to think it through, examine every angle before he commits it to words.

"I wasn't totally honest when I told people why we moved here," Yoshi starts. "We did move because Mom got a job, but that wasn't the main reason."

His eyes flicker to mine, and I nod for him to go on.

"My dad was a big deal at the TV station where he worked. He was known for his silly jokes, his weather ties, the costumes he'd wear. He used to be on the late news, but they actually moved him earlier because he was so popular. But the thing is, you can have all the gimmicks and tricks you want, but what you're ultimately judged on is correctly predicting the weather. Especially in Southern California, where there are so many severe weather incidents."

I realize that I'm holding my breath and try to let the air out slowly.

"All meteorologists make mistakes about the weather. You can't control the storm patterns, it's nature. But Dad felt all this pressure to get it right. All the time. He started taking it really hard when it was wrong, when he'd hear about outdoor festivals that got rained out when he said the chance of rain was low. The times the temperature reached dangerous highs and he hadn't told viewers to stay out of the sun. He started being extra cautious with his predictions so it wouldn't upset people. It's easier for people to deal with sunshine instead of rain than rain instead of sunshine."

"But that stuff isn't his fault." I can't help it. It's ridiculous to take the blame for the weather.

"You're right." He shrugs. "It's what everyone said. Nobody was mad at him. Well, except for the dumb people who wrote letters to the station complaining about their three-year-old's ruined birthday party."

My stomach tightens. "Doesn't he know that you're never supposed to read that stuff?"

"He does now."

I don't know why I thought that Yoshi was so laid-back about everything. Right now, he is anything but. I guess there are layers to him, just like there are to everyone. He's more than just a chill California boy.

"Is that why you guys moved here?" I ask.

Yoshi uses his glove to sweep away some of the snow that has drifted onto his lap. "Dad stopped going to work for a while after a wildfire started because of a lightning strike. It was too stressful. Southern California needed rain, and he was basically going crazy trying to find evidence that the rain was coming. And then, he just stopped leaving the house."

I press my palms against my legs to stop myself from doing something dumb. Like leaning over and hugging Yoshi.

"So I think part of the reason my parents chose to move to Flurry was because it would be a lower-stress job for him," Yoshi goes on. "I mean, what could be difficult about predicting snow or no snow? Except this year, all the town can talk about is the weather. People come and ask him about it on the street."

Yoshi's voice is still quiet. I think of all the times I've made comments about why his dad couldn't make better predictions.

"I'm so sorry."

Yoshi doesn't look up at me. "You didn't know. Maybe if I'd told you, you'd understand why I get so sensitive about these things."

For the millionth time, I wonder when I'm going to learn what Thierry always says: Everyone is dealing with their own heartaches and their own troubles, and just because they're smiling, doesn't mean they're okay.

"I promise to do better," I tell Yoshi.

"Thanks." He shrugs, and this time he looks at me and smiles. "So. I can't wait to see this festival in action."

"It's going to be epic."

We stand up. My heart feels very full. Together, we walk toward the Snowman Building booth. There's still lots to do, and tomorrow will be here before we know it.

Chapter Sixteen

I almost miss the opening of Flurry's Winter Festival because we're so busy at the inn. All of our rooms are full. Nobody canceled. Even the McAllistairs showed up. In the morning, I help Thierry in the kitchen, washing dishes and organizing the food based on when it will be served. By the time I'm done, I have to run over to our cottage to get dressed for the festival.

Snow fell all through the night, and it's still flurrying lightly. I put on my warmest jeans, my gray henley, a thick wool sweater, two pairs of socks, and snow boots. All set.

I make it in time for the first official event: the Snowshoe

Races. Maybe because I know how close we came to not having this event at all, I scream and cheer louder than I ever have before. Especially when Kyle's five-year-old sister wins the under-seven race. I can't believe that in the next few years, I'll be hollering for the littles as they compete. They'll either win every event or they'll be a total disaster. Either way, I'll be right here cheering them on.

After that, I find Lark, Yoshi, and Marcus. Yoshi is wide-eyed, taking it all in.

"This is so cool!" he exclaims. "Marcus and I are going to Top of the Mountain next to watch the cross-country skiing. Do you guys want to come?" he asks me and Lark.

We shake our heads. Lark and I have our traditions, which involve checking out the craft fair and then getting some of the snacks only available on Fridays. We say good-bye to Marcus and Yoshi, who we'll be seeing bright and early tomorrow. Then we roam around, stopping at all the craft booths. We try on bracelets and earrings, and I buy a handmade snow globe to give to the littles.

"Where to next?" I ask Lark. "I'm thinking I might need to sit down. I'm exhausted from all this walking. Want to try one of the fried snowflakes and sit on a bench?"

Lark gives me a look of utter contempt. "Seriously? How long have we been friends? Do you really think you need to fake being tired so that I don't feel badly about needing to sit down?"

I cough into my glove. "No, apparently I'm just out of shape. Because I'm actually exhausted."

"You're ridiculous," Lark says. "But I do want to try one of the fried snowflakes."

There are a dozen food trucks parked in a large circle with picnic tables and benches in the center. The whole area is lit up by the Flurry Trees and it brings tears to my eyes.

"It's so beautiful," I say, mostly to myself.

"It is," Lark says. "I'm really proud of you, you know. You made so much of this happen."

I think back to the conversation I had yesterday with Yoshi. And suddenly there's a part of me that's glad there's no sleigh ride this year. It's not that I didn't work hard as junior coordinator. I know I did. But this year was such a team effort, it wouldn't feel right to be in that sleigh by myself.

"We all made this happen," I respond.

"We did, but you brought it all together, Mia. I'm sorry I gave you such a hard time about suggesting all those ideas."

"You were right, though. I mean, it seems like the ideas will work, but it could have been a disaster."

"But it isn't."

"Nope." I smile.

We get in line for Bari's Fried Snowflakes, and I notice Kyle is working the cash register.

"Kyle must be in heaven." I laugh.

"It's the closest Bari will let him get to deep-frying dough. But he's wearing her down."

"Do you think he can get us extra fried snowflakes?"

"Definitely!"

And he does. Lark and I end up eating three each, and the stomachache is totally worth it.

*　　*　　*

Early the next morning, thirty seventh and eighth graders meet downtown to open both the Snow Carnival and the Snowman Building event. Yoshi gives everyone a quick orientation on what needs to be done for the Snow Carnival, and Lark explains the Snowman Building event.

The instructions are clear, and the volunteers are excited to help. So we open up the booths to the public.

The crowds are crazy right away. First, I hang around at the carnival, and I watch the little kids flood in to explore the booths, all of them eager and excited. I can't believe the aim that some of these kids have for the snowball tossing events. I might need to be extra careful at the snowball fight tomorrow. And the snowball bowling and golf are hilarious to watch.

As I leave, I wave at Yoshi, who is explaining to a little boy that he needs to let someone else into the snow chalet to play. Especially since there's already a line. But it looks like everything is under control.

So I move on to the Snowman Building booth, where a group of kids have apparently decided that they don't want to put the costumes on the ready-made snowmen; they want to use them as dress-up for taking pictures in the photo booth part.

"Is it okay that we're letting them?" Lark asks as two eighth graders bring out the background screen for a photo.

"I don't care," I admit. "I just want people to have fun."

"They are definitely having fun." Lark laughs and makes Kyle show me some of the ridiculous pictures he's taken so far.

"I love this so much," I gush. "Are the snowman building professionals behaving, also?"

"I think initially they were a little taken aback," Lark says, "but I've seen them using the selfie sticks with their own creations when nobody is watching. You should check out their stuff—they're just as cool as the ice sculptures."

"Are you sure they won't get mad at me for polluting their snowman building with all these costumes and props?" I'm only half joking. I mean, I think it's great, but my snowman building skills are much closer to the little kids' than the professionals.

"Go check out the northeast corner. Ask about the different versions of Mount Rushmore they've created and nobody will say boo about the little kids."

There's a large crowd around the four teams in the Mount Rushmore section, each one reimagining a modern-day memorial. From what I can see from the back of the crowd, there's an all-women's version, an African American version, and two I don't recognize.

"What are the two on the left?" I ask a man in front of me.

He turns and grins. "One is dedicated to the immigrants who built this country. And the other is WWE inspired."

A wrestler's monument?

I truly love this festival so much that I get teary-eyed.

I split my time between our areas, relieving people who need breaks or whose shifts are over, bringing box lunches for volunteers from the volunteer center. Wherever I go, I get high fives, and I feel so happy I could burst.

"Mia! Mia!" I'm finally taking a break on a snow-covered bench when Talulah and Tabitha descend on me.

"I can't get up," I complain to Shannon, which is a little ridiculous since she's just carted three kids around in a sled behind her. I'm grateful she doesn't call me on it.

"Come on, girls, let your sister relax," Shannon says, scooping Lilou up in her arms from the sled.

"Did you get fried snowflakes?" I ask the littles in a fake quiet voice.

Their eyes widen and their mouths open. "How do you fry a snowflake?"

"Tell your mom to take you to get some. And when you come back, I'll go through the Snow Carnival with you."

"There's a long line," Tabitha says.

"I think I can get you through."

And I do. After all, there has to be a benefit to having a crazy older sister.

* * *

Saturday passes in a blur. Before I know it, it's Sunday, and the marathon cross-country skiers are circling Flurry, and everyone is preparing for what we hope will finally be the World's Biggest Snowball Fight. The last two days have been better than I could possibly have imagined, but the one thing that has been bothering me is that I haven't really spent much time with Yoshi. And this is his first festival.

Luckily, the person I most want to see is now walking toward me wearing his bright blue, green, and yellow snowsuit, which makes him hard to miss.

"I feel like I haven't talked to you in days," Yoshi says when he reaches me.

"Was that on purpose? Did you get tired of me?" I tease, surprising myself.

"Never," he says, and it almost looks like he's serious.

"I feel bad because I wanted to show you around the festival, but now it's almost over."

"It's never too late to be my guide." Yoshi holds out his

gloved hand. "Plus, I've barely left the Snow Carnival, so I haven't seen that much."

Is this a *hold out your hand so we start moving* or a *hold out your hand because I want to hold your hand*? But then I push the worry aside and take his hand.

"Tell me that you've had the amazing fried snowflakes." I laugh.

Yoshi and I are holding hands.

"Oh my gosh. They were awesome. Fried snowflakes are my new favorite food."

Yoshi and I are holding hands.

"Did you get chestnuts?" I ask, and I hope that Yoshi doesn't hear the quiver in my voice. Because we're holding hands.

"Not yet. I was waiting for you."

It might be freezing cold outside, but I feel all warm and toasty. "Let's go get some chestnuts, then."

We each get two bags. I know it's too much, but the festival is about to end and I don't want to wait until next year to get a bag of roasted chestnuts.

"You up for a walk?" he asks when we've scarfed down most of the chestnuts. His smile is contagious, and I can't help but grin back. "Wait. But the snowball fight." Yoshi turns to me. "Are you okay if we don't do the snowball fight?"

"Are you willing to live with the possibility that we might be the difference between making it into the *Guinness World Records* or not?" I ask. "Because I definitely am."

Especially since it means that the rest of the festival will be less crowded.

We walk in silence, and all I can think about is the fact that I'm holding hands with a boy I like, and it's the final night of a really successful Flurry Winter Festival, and we won't have to move. It's like the whole world is perfect for a little while as the sun dips behind the trees.

Except, I know it isn't perfect. Nothing is. "I wanted to ask you how your dad is," I say to Yoshi.

Yoshi gives my hand a tiny squeeze. "He's doing okay," he says, his voice heavy with caution.

"Really?" I ask.

"I think that now that the snow is here, he's relieved. Plus, he and my mom really do love it here in Flurry."

"That sounds encouraging," I say, and he squeezes my hand again.

I think I really like holding hands.

"It is," he agrees. "He's also been seeing a therapist a couple of times a week, so that's been helpful. Thanks for asking."

"Of course," I say.

We begin to walk again, our hands still linked. Our conversation feels very grown-up, and part of me wants to dive down into the snow and make a giant snow angel just like I'm sure the littles have been doing all day. In the distance, I can hear the roar of the giant snowball fight.

"What happens when the snowball fight finishes?" Yoshi asks.

"There's a big closing ceremony," I say. I think of the sleigh ride that would normally happen then. But surprisingly, it doesn't hurt so much to think about missing out on the ride. And it actually gives me an idea.

"I want to make sure someone gets a picture of the five of us together," I say. "You, me, Marcus, Kyle, and Lark."

"Definitely," Yoshi says.

We walk on. "Do you remember the story I told you about Lark and the climbing wall?" I ask. We're heading past the food trucks, which are closed for business now. Soon we'll be in Snowflake Park, and once we're there . . .

Once we're there, I'll tell him how I feel, I promise myself.

"Of course I remember it. It's a great story."

I take a cue from Yoshi and pause, thinking about how I want to say all of this. I'm not sure it'll come out right, but I think it's important. "I feel like this festival was our climbing wall," I start. "I feel like we all had things we needed to prove to ourselves, and we all did them.

"I think for me, it was discovering that I could stand up for my ideas and see them come to life. It would have been so easy to give up or let the grown-ups take over, but I'm glad I stuck with it."

Yoshi nods, and without speaking, we move to a snow-covered bench and face each other. "I think for me it was becoming a part of things," he says. "And telling you about my dad."

I think about Marcus trying to find a place for himself in the school again, Kyle learning that he and Lark can be friends, even if they like each other in different ways, and Lark opening up to me about how she felt.

The sky isn't fully dark, so we can't see the stars, but I know they're there. It's a clear night, and if we can sit in the cold long enough, we'll be treated to an amazing sight.

Which means it's time to tell him.

"I have one more climbing-wall moment left," I say. I want to look in his eyes, but I'm not that brave. I know it will be okay if he doesn't feel the same way. I'll be sad, but we'll be able to make the friends thing work. But I really, really hope he does.

"Me too," Yoshi says. "You go first."

I take a deep breath. I can do this. "I wanted to tell you that I'm really glad you came to live in Flurry. That I've known for a while that you're really fun to hang out with, but that in the last two weeks, I've really gotten to see that." I take another breath. "Yoshi, I think I like you a lot." Noooo, that's not right. I cover my eyes with my gloves again, and then force myself to look at him. "Let me try again. I know I like you a lot. And I don't know how you feel about me but . . ."

Yoshi eyes are focused on mine. "I like you, too," he says. "A lot."

My whole face heats up.

"Like a lot a lot? Or—"

"Like a lot a lot," he admits.

"Really?" I ask. I know I shouldn't be arguing, but what if I'm misunderstanding him?

"Like enough that I want to ask you if I could kiss you—"

I lean forward, his words propelling me, and my lips

brush against his. I open my eyes, our faces so close together, and for a second I worry that he didn't want to kiss me or didn't want me to be the one to kiss him or . . .

But he smiles that tiny, hidden smile that I like so much, and then he leans forward until his lips hover over mine again. "Can we do that again?" he asks, and this time he takes the lead, and it's gentle and sweet. I don't know when he took off his gloves, but his warm hands are cupping my cold cheeks, and it makes the kiss that much more . . . everything.

Then we pull back, and the stars are lighting up the night sky. And I can't believe how lucky I am to live in a town like Flurry.

Tips on Making Your Own Great Photo Booth

Whether you're creating them for outdoors or indoors,
photo booths are easy and inexpensive to make on your own.
It could be a temporary setup for a birthday party (or a winter
festival!) or a more permanent setup in your home.

The Backdrop

Go simple: Use a blank wall or take pictures against a closed door. Taping wrapping paper to the wall can also create a uniform and temporary background, as can taping a large piece of fabric (or a sheet!) to the wall.

Go all out: Find a few large pieces of fabric and fold one end over about three inches and sew, or staple, down the line. Pick up a tension rod (available in the home section of most big stores) and use that to hang the fabric in doorways, over windows, etc. The rod can easily be taken down to change out the fabric. Be sure to ask an adult for help with these steps!

The Props

Go simple: Props such as fun hats and sunglasses can be purchased at most crafts stores, or online. If you want to make your own props, you can cut objects out of card stock or foam paper, and then tape or glue them to thin wooden sticks. Online, you can easily find patterns to trace for various kinds of hats, glasses, hair, lips, etc.

Go all out: Check out the thrift stores for costumes you can use for your photo booth. Carefully pop the lenses out of old glasses, and look for cool jackets, handbags, scarves, boas, ties, etc. Before wearing anything, make sure you clean it well!

The Signs

Go simple: Use the same paper you used to make the props, but write funny messages that can be held up. Arrows are always a popular choice, as are speech bubbles, thought bubbles, and hashtags.

Go all out: For signs that are a little less temporary, buy precut pieces of wood and paint them with chalk paint. With pieces of chalk or chalk markers, you can use the signs over and over again.

The Photos

Go simple: Prop up a camera, camera phone, or tablet, and use the timer. Take a few practice shots so you know exactly where people should stand. Otherwise, have a friend or family member be in charge of taking pictures.

Go all out: A selfie stick is the obvious choice if you're using a camera phone, but you can also purchase special boxes that will hold the camera phone in place to take the picture.

Most importantly, have fun!
When it comes to printing or posting the pictures,
you can keep them exactly as they are, or use photo editing
software that lets you mimic the effects of a real photo booth!
And remember to check with a grown-up and be responsible
when it comes to sharing photos anywhere.

Acknowledgments

Once again, I am awed by the number of people who are responsible for this book reaching your hands.

Aimee Friedman is the editor of my dreams. I learn so much about good writing from your edits and e-mails. Your support continues to be invaluable, but even more than that, your friendship is a true gift.

Rena Bunder Rossner is, as always, the type of agent every author dreams of having in their corner. Thank you for believing in me and my words.

The team at Scholastic has once again spoiled me for all others. Many, many thanks to David Levithan, Olivia Valcarce, Jael Fogle, Jennifer Rinaldi, Ann Marie Wong, Kristin Standley, Elizabeth Tiffany, Jody Corbett, and Natalia Remis.

My critique partners—Amy Pine, Megan Erickson, Lia Riley—are amazing and have kept me sane. I would be lost without you.

For this book, I'm grateful for the help especially of Jordy Heinrich, who was kind enough to share with me a tiny glimmer of what it's like to live with cerebral palsy. I made Lark as extraordinary as I could, but she still isn't nearly as fierce, strong, and generous as you. Thank you also to her parents, Inbar and Ken, and her fabulous siblings, Jonah and Noa

And finally, to my family. I was lucky enough to grow up celebrating winters in Ottawa with roasted chestnuts and BeaverTails, which more than made up for all the skiing and snow sports. Boundless gratitude to my mom; my sister, Jessica; and brother-in-law, Zane, who made possible a winter vacation so that I could re-create my snowy childhood.

And as always, to my husband, Josh, who is my biggest cheerleader, and to Jonah, Micah, and Toby, who are everything.

About the Author

Natalie Blitt is the author of *Carols and Crushes* and the young adult novel *The Distance from A to Z*. Originally from Canada, she now lives in the Chicago area with her husband and three sons, where she works at an education think tank. You can visit her online at natalieblitt.com.